"You're Every Bit As Beautiful As You Were Ten Years Ago...." Alexander Murmured. "I Remember..."

She wondered if he was remembering the way they'd stood here on the balcony, talking for hours. The first time he'd drawn her to him and kissed her.

The first time they'd made love.

"I remember this," he said, gazing around at the palace gardens. "You know what else I remember?"

"What?"

He turned to her, reached out to touch her arm. "This…"

It happened so quickly that she barely had a chance to think. One second she was standing beside Alex. The next, his lips were on hers and she was in his arms, the only place in the world where she'd ever truly felt she belonged.…

Dear Reader,

Welcome to book three of my ROYAL SEDUCTIONS series; the story of Alexander Rutledge and Princess Sophie.

As far as I'm concerned, there is no story more fun to write than a reunion tale. The process of working through all those past issues and emptying out the baggage to get to the heart of the relationship can be both exciting and heart-wrenching. And in Alex and Sophie's case, frustrating as all heck. I've been writing for a long time now and I've honestly never met two more stubborn people. There were times when I was sure they wouldn't make it, but like most of the people I write about, they surprised me in the end. I know you'll love them as much as I did.

Watch in January for the fourth installment in the ROYAL SEDUCTIONS series, the tale of Charles Mead, the Duke of Morgan Isle, and his feisty personal assistant, Victoria Houghton.

See you then!

Best,

Michelle

AN AFFAIR WITH THE PRINCESS

MICHELLE CELMER

Published by Silhouette Books
America's Publisher of Contemporary Romance

ISBN-13: 978-0-373-76900-1
ISBN-10: 0-373-76900-8

AN AFFAIR WITH THE PRINCESS

This edition published by arrangement with Harlequin Books S.A.

Visit Silhouette Books at www.eHarlequin.com

Printed in U.S.A.

Books by Michelle Celmer

Silhouette Desire

Playing by the Baby Rules #1566
The Seduction Request #1626
Bedroom Secrets #1656
Round-the-Clock Temptation #1683
House Calls #1703
The Millionaire's Pregnant Mistress #1739
The Secretary's Secret #1774
Best Man's Conquest #1799
**The King's Convenient Bride* #1876
**The Illegitimate Prince's Baby* #1877
**An Affair with the Princess* #1900

Silhouette Romantic Suspense

Running on Empty #1342
Out of Sight #1398

Silhouette Special Edition

Accidentally Expecting #1847

*Royal Seductions

MICHELLE CELMER

Bestselling author Michelle Celmer lives in southeastern Michigan with her husband, their three children, two dogs and two cats. When she's not writing or busy being a mom, you can find her in the garden or curled up with a romance novel. And if you twist her arm real hard you can usually persuade her into a day of power shopping.

Michelle loves to hear from readers. Visit her Web site, www.michellecelmer.com, or write her at P.O. Box 300, Clawson, MI 48017.

To my granddaughter Hannah.

One

Since she had been born into the royal family of Morgan Isle, there had been days when Princess Sophie Renee Agustus Mead felt restrained by her title.

Today was one of those days.

King Phillip sat behind his desk, in the palace office. She loved her brother to death, but there were times when the similarities between him and their late father were uncanny. The same jet-black hair and smoky gray eyes. The same towering height and lean, muscular build. The same *stubborn* streak.

Sophie on the other hand had inherited their father's quick and sometimes volatile temper. She took a deep breath and forced herself to remain calm, because she had learned years ago that blowing her top and pitching a fit only made Phillip dig his heels in deeper. "When you said I would be involved in the hotel project, Phillip, I had no idea my duties would include babysitting."

"No one knows this island like you do, Sophie. And if the architect is going to design a structure that complements the unique characteristics of our country, he's going to have to see it first."

She had wanted, had *hoped* that for the first time in her life the family would set aside their archaic traditions and allow her to take on a bit more than the royal responsibilities she sometimes grew so tired of. Something slightly more challenging than planning parties, attending charity functions and playing goodwill ambassador.

Both Phillip and their half brother, Prince Ethan, had assured her that if she stuck to the royal program without complaint, she would be involved in the business of the hotel chain the family had recently purchased. And in light of her current *assignment,* she couldn't help but feel she was getting, as the Americans liked to say, the raw end of the deal.

But if she refused, she wouldn't put it past Phillip to cut her out of the project completely. What he really wanted was to see Sophie settle down and start squeezing out royal heirs. With the recent birth of his son, Frederick, and the pregnancy of Ethan's wife, Lizzy, suddenly everyone was looking at her as though to say, *okay, now it's your turn.* But she wasn't ready. She wasn't sure if she *ever* would be.

"Fine," she said with a smile. "I'll do it. Although I'm not crazy about the idea of spending two weeks with a stranger."

Phillip relaxed back in his chair, satisfied now that he had gotten what he wanted. "Well then, you'll be relieved to know that he's not."

"I don't recall ever meeting any American architect."

"It was years ago, and when you met him, he wasn't an architect yet. He came home with me from university and spent the holidays."

Sophie's heart dropped so hard and fast that she could swear she felt it split in two and hit the balls of her feet. He couldn't possibly mean…

"I seem to recall," Phillip continued, "the two of you getting along somewhat famously."

If he was referring to the man she suspected he was, famously didn't begin to describe those two weeks. But there was no way Phillip could have known about that. Only her mother, who unbeknownst to Sophie had been listening in on her phone conversations, knew the extent of Alex's and her "friendship."

Behind her the office door opened and she turned to see her half brother, Prince Ethan, enter the room. Behind him appeared a man who, despite ten years apart, was still strikingly familiar. In fact, he hadn't changed much at all. He wore his pale brown hair in the same short, meticulous style and his deep-set eyes were the same piercing, hypnotizing blue. Eyes she had once hoped to spend an entire lifetime gazing into.

Alexander Rutledge, the only man she had ever loved.

Typically reserved, Phillip rose from his chair to greet his friend with an enthusiastic, "Alex, welcome back to Morgan Isle!"

Alex stepped forward, a smile breaking out across his handsome, chiseled features. He was dressed just like her brothers, in an expensive-looking suit and shoes polished to a gleaming shine. And he was standing so close that Sophie could reach out and touch him, yet he didn't even seem to notice her there. Had he forgotten about her?

Something that felt like a boulder settled in the pit of her stomach. As if it mattered after all this time. He was nothing to her.

Alex gripped the king's hand and gave it a firm shake. "Phillip. It's been far too long. How have you been?"

"Busy. I'm a family man now."

"I've heard. I'm anxious to meet your wife and son."

"You must remember my sister," Phillip said, gesturing her way. "Princess Sophie."

Sophie's heart soared up to lodge in her throat. This was it. The first time they would share words in over ten years. Ten years in which barely a day passed when she hadn't thought of him.

Alex turned in her direction, greeting her with a perfunctory nod, wearing a polite smile that didn't quite reach his eyes. "Your Highness. It's good to see you again."

That was it? That was all she got? *Good to see you again?*

She was appalled to feel the beginnings of tears sting the corners of her eyes. She bit down hard on the inside of her cheek and forced herself to smile. "Alex," she said, her voice surprisingly even considering she was trembling from the inside out.

"I understand you're to be my guide for the duration of my stay," he said, and she honestly couldn't tell how he felt about that. Nary a trace of any discernible emotion showed on his face. Had he forgotten about her? About those two amazing weeks?

"Yes, I am. However, I was just now informed, and haven't had time to create an itinerary. You won't mind if the tour doesn't officially begin until tomorrow morning."

"Of course not." He wasn't rude or unpleasant or even cold. Just…indifferent. But how had she expected him to react? Did she think he would sweep her up in his arms and declare his undying love for her? As far as she knew, he was a happily married family man, like Phillip.

"Sophie," Phillip said, "could you please show Alex to the guest suite?"

"Of course." As if she had a choice. "The garden suite?" she asked, and Phillip nodded.

"Take some time to settle in," Phillip told Alex. "I'll take you on a tour of the palace later this afternoon. Oh, and, Sophie, I'd like to see the itinerary when you're done."

"Of course. I'll fax it to you later this evening."

"Why don't you just bring it with you to dinner tonight?"

She'd had no idea that she was expected to have dinner at the palace. She usually ate at her own residence on the palace grounds.

"Is that an invitation?" she asked her brother, smiling sweetly, because she knew, Phillip didn't invite. He demanded.

"I thought it would be nice that we all be here to welcome our guest." He worded it as a suggestion, but what he really meant was be there or else.

"The usual time?" she asked.

He nodded.

"Fine, I'll see you then." She turned to their *guest.* "If you'll follow me, I'll show you to your suite."

He gestured to the door. "After you. Your Highness."

She wasn't a self-conscious person. Not even when it came to her physical appearance. She had been blessed with good genes, and at thirty was still tall and very slim and nothing had yet begun to sag. But for some reason knowing that Alex was behind her was making her incredibly self-conscious. And as they walked to the stairs the lack of conversation stretched like a mile-wide void between them. But if there was one thing she had learned in all of her years as goodwill ambassador, it was the art of small talk.

"How was your trip?" she asked him as they climbed the stairs to the second floor, where the guest suites were located.

"Tiring," he said. "I'd forgotten what a long flight it is from the U.S. to Morgan Isle."

He stayed to the side and one step behind her. Which was proper, but it still annoyed her. She wanted to see his face. Relearn his features. Not that she'd ever really forgotten. In fact, it was probably better that she not let herself get caught up in what they used to have. That was a long time ago. Although it was a wonder he wasn't bitter for the way things had ended. Of course, for all she knew, the instant they were alone he might read her the riot act. And could she blame him? It was she who had ended things without an explanation. She who refused his calls and sent his letters back unopened.

But what choice did she have? The decision had been taken out of her hands.

"The palace hasn't changed much since I was here last," Alex noted.

"Nothing much around here ever changes."

"I see that," he said, and something in his tone made the surface of her skin tingle. "You're still as beautiful as you were ten years ago."

She waited for the qualifier to that statement, something like, *and still as coldhearted.* But when she realized he was sincere, her stubborn heart jumped back up in her throat.

"You look the same, too," she conceded, disconcerted by how vulnerable it made her feel. Uncomfortable. And she rarely felt uncomfortable around *anyone.*

As they passed the doorway to the residence she

nodded to the guard on duty, then took Alex in the opposite direction, into the guest wing to the first door on the left.

"I believe this is the same suite you stayed in the last time you were here." In fact, she knew it was. She'd spent enough time there with him in those two weeks to remember quite precisely.

She opened the door and gestured him inside, following a few steps behind. "As you probably remember, this is the sitting room, and there's also a sleeping chamber and bath."

"I remember," he said, sounding almost wistful. Was he thinking the same thing that she was? Was he remembering the way they stood on the balcony overlooking the gardens and talked for hours? The first time he drew her to him and kissed her.

Did he remember the first time they made love?

Never before or since had another man made her feel more loved and accepted. More special. But that was a long time ago and so much had changed since then. *She* had changed.

"I remember this," he said, gazing around the room. "You know what else I remember?"

"What?"

He turned to her, reached out to touch her arm. "This…"

It happened so quickly that she barely had a chance to process it. One second she was standing beside Alex, and the next she was in his arms, the only place in the world that she'd ever felt she truly belonged. Her first instinct was to push him away, but instead she went weak all over. Then his lips were touching hers, as naturally as if they had never spent a day apart.

She knew this was wrong in more ways than she could count, not the least of which that he was married, but as the kiss deepened, as she tasted the familiar flavor of his mouth, breathed in the scent of his skin and hair, there wasn't a thing she could do, or would even *want* to do, to stop him.

Well, that was easy, Alex mused as Sophie all but dissolved in his arms. He tunneled his fingers through the soft black ribbons of hair that fell loose around her face. She tasted sweet and exciting and sexy. He nibbled her lower lip lightly wondering if that still drove her nuts, and was answered with a shiver and a soft moan of pleasure.

And here he thought seducing her was going to be a time-consuming, tedious task. And why wouldn't he? After she vowed her eternal love for him, then dumped him with no explanation.

As though reading his mind, she tensed. He felt her hands flatten against his chest. And because he didn't want to push too far to soon, he didn't try to stop her when she backed away from him.

She stared at him with eyes the color of a storm blowing inland off the Atlantic Ocean. Deep, turbulent gray. Her cheeks were pink and he could see the flutter of her pulse at the base of her long, graceful throat. And to be honest he was feeling a bit breathless himself. Despite everything that had happened, the way she had used him, she still turned him on.

Which would make using *her* that much more satisfying.

"Why did you do that?" she asked, her voice shaky.

"Sophie, I've been wanting to do that for ten years."

She took another step away, pressing the backs of her fingers to her lips, as though his touch had seared her. "I could call a guard and have you detained for assault."

He just smiled, because he knew she would never do that. She may have been self-centered, spoiled and manipulative, but she wasn't vindictive. At least, not back then. "But you won't, because that would be a lie. You wanted it as much as I did."

He could see from her reaction that he was right, but he also knew that she wouldn't let him off the hook that easily.

"I'm not sure what kind of woman you think I am, but I don't involve myself with married men."

Is that why she looked so scandalized? Not that she was in any position to be questioning his character. Or morals.

He folded his arms across his chest. "I guess you haven't heard. I've just been through the nastiest divorce in recorded history."

That information seemed to sober her. "No, I hadn't. I'm sorry to hear that."

The odd thing was that she looked truly sorry.

And here he thought the only person she cared about was herself. But he didn't believe for a second that she had made some startling transformation over the past ten years. He didn't doubt that sooner or later the real Sophie would make a grand entrance. And when she did, he would be ready.

"I suppose that's what happens when you marry someone you don't love," he said. "I guess you had the right idea."

She looked confused.

"You didn't love your fiancé, and you didn't marry him. In fact, Phillip tells me that you've never been married."

"No, I haven't." She glanced toward the door, then back to him. "I should leave you to unpack."

"Running away again, Sophie?"

A frown furrowed the space between her brows. "I have to ask you from now on to please keep your hands to yourself. Next time I *will* alert security."

No, she wouldn't, but for now he would play along. Let her think that she had the upper hand. It was all a part of the game. "Of course, Your Highness. I apologize for my…inappropriate behavior."

"Dinner is in the main dining room at seven sharp. Do you remember where that is?"

"I'm sure I can find my way."

She nodded. "If you have any questions or need anything, there's a directory beside the phone. The kitchen is open twenty-four hours. You also have a full wet bar."

"Thank you."

She nodded, then turned and left, closing the door firmly behind her.

Maybe this wouldn't be quite as easy as he thought, but he'd always enjoyed a challenge. The harder he worked for something, the more satisfying the payoff when he finally got it.

He was taking a risk, putting his personal and professional relationship with Phillip on the line. The family firm, Rutledge Design, was unrivaled in North America, but they needed this credit to their portfolio if they were going to take the company international. Just as his father had always dreamed of doing but never accomplished himself.

And hadn't Alex always done what his father expected of him? He'd been dead and buried for three years now and Alex was *still* trying to please him.

Which in part was to blame for the mother of all divorces that Alex had just endured. An inevitability, he supposed, when a man married for convenience instead of love. To please his family instead of himself. In his entire life he'd met only one woman who had ever understood the pressures of living up to the expectations of others.

That woman was Sophie. When Alex had come to stay at the palace during a college break, he and Sophie had immediately connected. When he was with her, Alex had felt as though he could let down his guard and just be himself.

Little had he known it was just a game to her.

Seeing her again brought it all back—the confusion and humiliation. So what better time than now to get a little revenge? Give her a taste of her own medicine.

Seduce her, make her fall in love with him, then dump her, just as she'd done to him.

Two

Sophie was still trembling as she descended the stairs and headed for the back entrance. What she needed right now was to be alone. She needed time to process what had just happened, and figure out why it had scared her half to death.

But as she was rounding the corner just before the outer door, she ran into Ethan, who was also on his way out.

"Heading home?" he asked, holding the door for her.

She forced a smile. "I have an itinerary to plan." Since leaving Alex's suite, she had felt chilled to the bone, and the bright afternoon sunshine and warm breeze felt soothing on her face and arms.

They walked together toward his black, convertible Porsche.

"You realize you'll never get a car seat in that thing," she teased.

"Don't remind me," he said, pulling his keys from his pants pocket. Although everyone in the family had their own custom Rolls-Royce and driver, Ethan still preferred to drive himself most days. And he rarely used the services of a bodyguard.

They stopped by the driver's-side door. "Our guest all settled in?" he asked.

"Yes, all settled in."

"He seems like a nice guy."

"Yes, very nice." A little *too* nice, actually. Far too…*friendly.* And she didn't trust him.

Ethan narrowed his eyes at her, looking so much like Phillip that it was almost eerie. "Is something wrong?"

It amazed her that, despite having only learned of each other's existence last year, he could read her so well. Must have been some sort of paternal bond that linked them despite being only half siblings. And at a time like now, it was incredibly inconvenient.

"I'm fine," she told him, but could tell he didn't believe her. She prayed silently that he would drop it. He didn't of course.

"I know what's going on here, Sophie."

She swallowed hard. How could he possibly know about her relationship with Alex? Unless Alex had told him. Which he had *no* right doing. It was between him and Sophie.

He put a hand on her arm. "I understand how you feel."

"You do?"

"I felt the same way when I started in the hotel business. I wanted to be the one in control. The one calling the shots. But it was easier for me in the sense that I didn't have a well-meaning family trying to hold me back."

He was talking about the business, not her and Alex's complicated past. She was so relieved she felt faint. Although, if there was anyone in the world she would feel comfortable confiding in, other than her sister-in-law, Hannah, it would be Ethan. But as was her way, she preferred to figure out things on her own.

"You want more responsibility," Ethan continued. "More than shuttling guests around the island."

She shrugged. "But that just isn't the way things are done in this family. I'm a princess and my royal duties must come first."

He gave her arm an affectionate squeeze. "Although I don't have a lot of influence with Phillip, I am working on it. But honestly, between the hotel and the baby coming, I barely have a free minute."

"Is Lizzy feeling better? She has to be close to her fourth month now."

"She still has terrible morning sickness. She had hoped to keep working until her eighth month. You know how restless she gets when she's not busy, but she can barely crawl out of bed in the morning. She tries to eat but can't keep anything down and the doctor is concerned that she's losing a dangerous amount of weight. I hate to leave her alone all the time while I'm working, so I'm considering moving us into the palace for a while. At least until she's feeling better. Or gives birth. Whichever comes first I guess."

"I think that would be a good idea, and I'm sure Phillip will be thrilled. You know how he feels about keeping the family close. Although I have to say I'm a bit surprised. This coming from the man who swore he would *never* live in the palace?"

He grinned and shrugged. "I guess I never expected to feel at home here. Or to think of Phillip as family. It's amazing how quickly things change."

Wasn't that the truth. Just this morning it had been business as usual, and now it felt as though her entire life had just been turned upside down.

He unlocked his car. "Guess I should go. Can I give you a lift home?"

"No, thanks. It's such a beautiful day." And it was only a brisk five-minute walk if she followed the stone path. "Give Lizzy my best. And tell her if she needs help with anything, all she has to do is ask."

"I will." He gave her a quick hug and a peck on the cheek, then climbed into his car. Sophie started down the path toward home, watching as he zipped out of the lot and drove away.

It seemed as though lately everyone she knew was settling down and starting a family. People who, like her, swore they would never give up their freedom. Ethan was right, things did change quickly. But for her, certain things, things like wanting a husband and family, would never change. She'd spent her entire life struggling for her freedom, and she wasn't going to give that up.

Not for anyone.

Referencing files of itineraries she had created in the past few years, Sophie was able to whip up a suitable plan for the next two weeks well before dinner. It was something of a challenge considering the average guest stayed several days. Thankfully, though, several of those afternoons Alex would spend with Phillip doing the usual guy things, like fishing and golfing. But for the remainder of the trip, he was basically all hers.

She was printing off copies for herself, Phillip and the social secretary when her butler knocked on her office door. "Yes, Wilson."

He bowed his head. "Sorry to interrupt, Miss, but you have a visitor."

A visitor? She wasn't expecting anyone today. How would they even get past the guards at the main gate without her consent? "Who?"

"A Mr. Rutledge."

Just as it had in Phillip's office earlier that day, her heart took a deep dive downward. Bloody hell, why did it keep doing that? And what was Alex doing here? At *her* house? He had no right to just barge in on her.

She considered ordering Wilson to tell Alex that she was busy and didn't have time for guests, but if she refused to see him, he would realize how much his stunt back in the palace had rattled her. And if she had to spend the next two weeks carting him around the island, showing vulnerability was not an option.

She would *have* to see him.

"Show him to the study. I'll be down in just a minute."

Wilson nodded and disappeared into the hall. Sophie took a long, deep breath and rose from her chair. She had no reason to be nervous, but as she crossed the room her legs felt weak and trembly. *Get a grip, Sophie.*

If she had this reaction every time she saw him, this was going to be a very long and exhausting two weeks.

She stopped in front of the mirror in the upstairs hallway and checked her reflection. She looked as pale as death. She smoothed her hair and pinched a little color back into her cheeks, reminding herself once again that Alex was no longer a man of consequence. That part of her life was over. Now he was merely a business associate.

She descended the stairs slowly, her heart creeping further up her throat with every step. Alex was in the study by the window, gazing out across the pristinely manicured lawn. He seemed lost in thought, a million miles away, and it struck her again how handsome he was. How familiar. And for a moment she gave herself permission to just look at him. And remember.

"Thanks for seeing me," he said, nearly startling her out of her skin.

Bloody hell! No matter how collected she tried to be, he always managed to throw her off kilter. "I thought you understood that the tour would begin tomorrow."

"I know, but I wanted to see you." He turned to her, looking humbled. "So I could apologize."

Well, this was unexpected. "There's really no need."

"Yes, there is. What I did was wrong. I guess…" He shrugged. "I guess I just got caught up in the past. And I assumed, or maybe *hoped,* that you felt the same way. That you missed me as much as I've missed you."

He looked sincere, but something in his words didn't ring true. In her world, men did not offer up their feelings like a neatly wrapped gift. So naturally, she couldn't escape the suspicion that he was saying what he *thought* she wanted to hear.

Or had thirty years living in the midst of nothing but emotionally vacant men left her jaded?

"And since you obviously don't feel that way," he continued. "I just wanted to say that I was sorry, and assure you that it won't happen again."

Was that disappointment she just felt? Surely she didn't *want* it to happen again.

But the memory of his lips pressed to hers, his hands cupping her face, fingers tangling in her hair, made her scalp tingle and her knees even weaker than they already felt. But that was just physical. Emotionally she had no place for a man like him in her life. Not even temporarily. "Apology accepted."

"I'm not usually so impulsive. Or reckless. It's a

lousy excuse, but going through this divorce really has me off my game."

She stepped a little farther into the room. "I'm sorry to hear that."

"If you're not busy, I was hoping we could take a while to talk, get reacquainted. Because it seems we're stuck with each other."

With the itinerary completed, there was really nothing pressing on her schedule, and it was still several hours until dinner. Besides, it might make things a bit less awkward. It wouldn't kill her to give him the benefit of the doubt and grant him the concession of a simple conversation. If only she could shake the feeling that he had ulterior motives.

For now she would give him what he wanted, but she would tread lightly, and at the first sign of trouble she would put him in his place.

"Would you like a drink?" Sophie asked, and Alex knew she was as good as his. It might take a bit longer than he expected to break down the barriers, but it was only a matter of time now. She looked and acted tough, but he knew what it took to make a woman melt. His ability to accurately read the subtle emotional cues of the opposite sex and respond accordingly was something of a gift. It was the only reason his marriage had lasted as long as it had. Although in retrospect, that hadn't been one of his brightest moves. He should have left her a long time ago. Or even better, never married her in the first place.

"Mineral water, if you have it," he said.

"With lime?"

"Please."

He expected her to call her butler, instead she walked to the bar and poured the drinks herself. A mineral water for him, and a glass of white wine for herself. She carried the glass to him, and when he took it, she gestured to the couch.

"Please, sit."

She waited until he was seated then took a place on an adjacent chair. She wore a gauzy, cotton dress that accentuated her long, willowy form. She had always struck him as more of an earthy, free spirit than a royal. Back then she had felt stifled and suffocated by her title, yet now she seemed to embrace it.

He wondered if she was still as self-centered and spoiled.

"Nice house," he said. "I'm surprised you don't still live in the palace with the rest of the family."

"I like my privacy."

"Have you lived here long?"

"I moved in after my mother passed away."

Which made sense. He couldn't see her parents allowing her to live in her own place. He remembered her parents to be very strict and controlling. Which was probably part of the thrill of their affair. That element of danger. Had she been discovered sneaking into his suite every night, he'd have been booted out on his ear and most likely banished from the country for life.

She sipped her wine and asked, "How was it that you and my brother reconnected?"

She was asking polite, benign questions. Holding him at arm's length. But that was fine. He had two weeks to work his way under her skin. For now he would play along.

"We've kept in touch occasionally over the years, and he remembered that I was interested in taking my firm international. So when he needed someone to design the fitness center, I was the first one he called. He and Ethan looked at my portfolio and liked what they saw. When Phillip learned of my less-than-amicable divorce, he suggested I take a few weeks off and come visit. And I have to admit, this is the most relaxed I've been in months."

"You own the architectural firm?"

He nodded. "Since my father passed three years ago."

"I'm so sorry to hear that. How is your mother?"

"Good. She lives in upstate New York now, near my sister."

"And you're still based in Manhattan?"

"I got the apartment in the settlement. She got the mansion upstate." Then he added, "If I sound bitter, it's because I am."

She nodded sympathetically. It couldn't hurt to play the pity card, even though the truth of the matter was, the monstrosity his ex had insisted on buying had never felt like home to him. He spent the majority of his time in the city, commuting upstate on the weekends to see her. However, over the past year he'd been making the trip less and less. At times only once a month.

When he'd learned of her infidelity, he'd been more relieved than angry. Finally he had an out.

That, however, hadn't stopped her from trying to bleed him dry.

He took a sip of his drink and set it on the table beside him. "So, I take it from your reaction in Phillip's office that you had no idea I was coming to visit."

"No, I didn't."

"I remember how much you hated being left out of the loop. You used to say that you felt like window dressing."

"I'm surprised you remember that."

He leaned forward slightly. "I remember lots of things, Princess."

He could see her working that one through, but before she had the opportunity to reply, her butler appeared in the open doorway. "The King to see you, Miss."

Alex and Sophie both rose from their seats as Phillip stepped into the room. When Phillip saw him there, he smiled. "There you are, Alex."

"I'm sorry," Alex said. "I didn't realize you were looking for me."

"Nothing urgent," Phillip assured him. "I just wanted to be sure that you were all settled in."

"I am. I have everything I could possibly need."

"Alex thought it would be a good idea for us to get

acquainted," Sophie said, with no hint of the nature of her and Alex's true relationship. Or, *ex*-relationship.

"I'm actually here because I need to have a word with my sister," Phillip said. "If you'll excuse us for a moment, Alex."

"Of course. I should get back to the palace anyway. I have a few phone calls to make before dinner. It was nice talking to you, Sophie."

"You, too," she said, with one of those smiles that was a little too indifferent to be genuine. Was that for his benefit or her brother's?

She turned to her butler. "Please show our guest out."

"I guess I'll see you at dinner," Alex said, nodding to both Sophie and Phillip, then he followed the butler to the door.

Why, he wondered, would Phillip come all the way to her residence instead of just picking up the phone?

He had the distinct feeling he would eventually find out.

Three

Alex's cell phone rang as he was walking back to the palace. He checked the display and saw that it was his attorney, Jonah Livingston, who also happened to be his best friend. Over the years that had proved to be both a good and a bad thing. There wasn't much about his life Jonah didn't know. And he'd been known to give Alex hell when he thought he was acting in a manner contrary to his best interests. Professional *and* personal. And he was usually right. Like the day of Alex's wedding, when Jonah implored him to take a step back and think about what he was doing. He tried to convince Alex that marrying someone he didn't love was far worse than not getting married at all. And eventually Alex's father would give him his job back and write him back into the will.

Now Alex wished he had listened.

He almost dreaded answering the call. When he left for Morgan Isle, everything pertaining to the divorce had been settled, or so they believed, but his ex hadn't actually signed on the dotted line yet. It wouldn't be the first time she'd agreed to the terms, then changed her mind at the last minute and lashed out with more demands.

They had been going back and forth with this for more than a year now. A long, tedious year he would have much rather spent forgetting he was ever married and starting with a clean slate. He just wanted it to be over. And now he needed to know if it was.

Just before the call went to voice mail he flipped open the phone. "This better be good news."

Jonah chuckled. "Hello, to you, too. I trust you're having a good time."

"I'd be having a better time if you had some good news. Did you hear from the divorce attorney?"

"I just got off the phone with her."

"And?"

"You want to know what she said?"

He closed his eyes and sighed heavily. "This is so not the time to mess with me, Jonah."

Jonah laughed. "You can relax, buddy. This time it's definitely good news."

"She signed?"

"In her lawyer's office yesterday, with plenty of

witnesses to make it binding. As of this morning the papers are officially signed and filed and you, my friend, are a free man."

He should have felt some level of regret or even sadness, but all he could manage to feel was relieved. "That is *very* good news."

"She's going by the apartment tomorrow to pick up the rest of her things."

"And you'll be there?"

"Me and three of my associates, just to be safe. We won't take our eyes off her for a second. She won't take anything that she isn't supposed to. And if she tries, I won't hesitate to get the police involved."

He was just glad Jonah was handling this, so he didn't have to. If he never saw her again, that would be fine with him. In fact, he preferred it that way. "You think it will come to that?"

"She may be manipulative and greedy, but she's not stupid. And honestly, I think she's as ready for this to be over as you are."

"Guess I should have listened all those years ago when you warned me not to marry her."

"Yeah, but when do you ever listen to me? Which reminds me, how are things going with your princess?"

"She's not my princess," he said, then added with a grin, "Not yet anyway."

"I hope you know what you're doing."

"Don't I always?"

He laughed. "Honestly, *no.* That's why you have me. To keep you out of trouble."

"Well, this time I'm in total control."

"Like I haven't heard that before."

"Don't worry," he told Jonah. "This time it's different. I know *exactly* what I'm doing."

"Sophie, this behavior is completely inappropriate," Phillip said after Alex left and they were alone.

There he went with the stern look again. Sophie had to make an effort not to roll her eyes. Would he never learn? "What is it that you find inappropriate, Phillip?"

"Don't play dumb."

"Let's pretend for a second that I am dumb. Because, frankly, I have no clue why you're in such a snit."

"Your being alone in *your* residence with *my* guest."

"You can't be serious." Where in bloody hell did he get off telling her who she could and couldn't invite into her home? She was sick to death of everyone thinking they had the right to tell her how to live her own life. "Are you forgetting that *you're* the one who stuck me with him for two weeks? Not to mention that who I choose to invite into *my* house is none of your damned business."

"He's not one of your disposable distractions. This is business, Sophie. If you expect to be treated like an equal, you have to act the part."

She couldn't deny that his words stung. Wasn't it just like her brother to assume the worst. "He was at my home, so you just assume I'm sleeping with him? He was here, what, *ten* minutes? I certainly don't waste any time, do I?"

"I'm just making sure you understand my feelings on this."

If she didn't know any better, she would think that Phillip knew about her complicated past with Alex. But if he did, he surely would have said something about it years ago. He'd never held back before when he disapproved of her conduct.

And she was tired of feeling as though she was living her life under a microscope.

She had half a mind to sleep with Alex just to spite him. But what would that prove other than the fact that he was right about her?

She walked toward the door. "I have to dress for dinner now."

Her way of saying, "Get the hell out," without actually saying it. And wonder of all wonders, he actually acquiesced. He walked to the door, then stopped and turned back to her. "You know that I only do things that I feel are in your best interest."

"I know that, Phillip."

And that was the problem. Everyone thinking they knew what was better for her than she did.

Thankfully, Alex was seated at the opposite end of the table from Sophie during dinner. And although the entire family was there—Phillip and his wife, Queen Hannah, Ethan and Lizzy, who was looking decidedly green, and their cousin Charles, the family attorney—the tone of conversation was more business than personal. They talked mainly of the hotel and the plans for the new fitness center Alex's firm would be designing, and when the purchase of the property would be final.

"It's as good as ours," Charles assured them. "Old man Houghton has no choice but to sell. Considering the financial ruin he's facing, what we're offering is a gift. He would be a fool not to take it."

"The existing building will have to come down immediately," Phillip said.

"Demolition has already been scheduled," Ethan told him.

"But it's such a beautiful old building," Hannah said wistfully. "Isn't there a way to salvage it?"

"Although it may be aesthetically pleasing," Alex explained. "The building is so old and structurally unsound that it would be more cost-effective to tear it down and put a new building in its place."

"What about all of the employees who will be out of work when it shuts down?" Lizzy asked, though it was obvious, despite her attempts to join the conversation, that she felt awful. She only picked at her food and often reached over to clutch Ethan's hand for support.

"We'll hire as many as we can," Ethan said. "A deal is already in the works to have Houghton's daughter, Victoria, brought in as a manager. It's the one thing he's insisted on."

"But is she trustworthy?" Charles asked, because protecting the family was his duly appointed task. "Despite the generous nature of our offer, Houghton hasn't been shy about his negative feelings toward the family. What if he wants his daughter involved so she can make trouble?"

"We thought of that," Ethan said. "Until we know we can trust her, we're going to have her work in your office, so you can keep an eye on her. Once it's determined that her loyalties lie with us, she'll be transferred to the hotel. You can find a spot for her, can't you?"

Charles nodded. "No problem."

As the dessert plates were being cleared, Lizzy, now as pale as a ghost, excused herself to go lie down and Ethan left with her to be both moral and, apparently, physical support.

Hannah watched with concern, and when they were gone, said to Phillip, "She's not looking well. I was sick in my first few months, but never that bad."

"I'm concerned, too," Phillip admitted. "But according to Ethan, there isn't anything the doctor can do for her. She just has to ride it out. I told Ethan they didn't have to be here for dinner, but he said Lizzy insisted." He glanced over to Sophie. "She's strong-willed."

She flashed him a wry smile. "To survive in this family you have to be."

Hannah shot them both a look that seemed to say, *behave, you two,* then said, "If you'll all excuse me, I have to go check on Fredrick."

As she stood, so did the men at the table.

"I'll go with you," Phillip said.

Charles looked at his watch. "I should push off, as well. Hot date tonight."

Sophie rolled her eyes. "Is there ever a night when you don't have a hot date?"

Charles just grinned.

"Sophie," Phillip said, "why don't you take Alex on a walk through the gardens?"

"Oh, yes!" Hannah agreed. "It's lovely at sunset."

Either it was a show of faith on Phillip's part or he was sending some insanely mixed messages. But it wasn't as though she had anything better to do.

Ethan had Lizzy to care for, Phillip and Hannah were off to spend time with their infant son and Charles was going on a date. Sophie couldn't help feeling she'd just been handed the booby prize.

But because she was the goodwill ambassador, and God knows she had played this game a million times before, she turned to Alex and smiled. "Would you care to take a walk in the gardens, Alex?"

He returned the smile, and she could swear she saw the spark of a twinkle in his eye. "I would love to, Your Highness."

They all went their separate ways, and Sophie led Alex outside, with the undeniable sneaking suspicion that this was some sort of test. That Phillip would be watching. She wondered what he would do if he saw her plant a wet one on Alex right there amid the rose and hydrangea bushes.

The light was just beginning to fade and the sun sat like a shimmering orange globe just above the tree line in the cloudless evening sky. The heat of the day had begun to fade and a cool breeze blew from the north, rustling the leaves and spreading the faint aroma of moss. Sophie led Alex down the flagstone path that wound its way carelessly through a long stretch of flower gardens that had become the pride of the royal family. Every year it grew and expanded as new species of plants and flowers were added. Hybrids mostly, and many that had been bred by the palace gardener himself.

She pointed out the different varieties, giving both their common and scientific names, but Alex seemed distant.

"Am I boring you?" she finally asked.

He grinned. "No, sorry. I guess I'm still processing everything that I've seen this evening."

"What do you mean?"

"It's been so long, I'd nearly forgotten what it was like to have a family dinner."

"Well, the topic usually doesn't revolve around business. Typically it's everyone sticking their noses into everyone else's business. But in sort of a good way, I guess."

"Even so, it was remarkably…cohesive."

She supposed that it was. They were a close family. Now, anyway. They didn't used to be. The only family dinners she and Phillip ever shared with their parents was during holidays or royal functions. Their mother and father led very separate lives. From not just each other, but their children, as well. Child rearing in their opinion was better left to the nannies. Sophie often used to feel that it was her and Phillip against the world.

"I take it you and your wife didn't share dinner," she said, realizing immediately the personal nature of the question, but it was too late to take it back. And she was at least a little curious about his life.

He shook his head. "Not for a long time."

He looked so sad, she couldn't help but feel sorry for him. And she found herself asking, "Do you have children?"

He shook his head. "That was a major sore spot. She wanted them, I didn't."

That surprised her. Ten years ago he had seemed eager to start a family, but then, so had she. If the family she would have been starting was his, that is. Now, there didn't seem much point. She couldn't imagine finding a man she could care enough about to bear his children. She no longer had the energy to look. The men she passed the time with these days were, as Phillip had pointed out, nothing more than a temporary distraction.

"But I wasn't being entirely honest," he admitted. "I wanted kids. Just not with her."

So why did he marry her?

"I know what you're thinking," he said. "Why marry a woman I didn't want to start a family with?"

Whoa, that was weird. And she couldn't stop herself from asking, "Why did you?"

"Pressure from my family. I was young and naive and thought that in time I would learn to love her. By the time I realized that you have to like someone before you can learn to love them, it was too late."

That was the difference between them, she supposed. She knew that she would never fall in love with the man her parents had chosen for her. That only happened in fairy tales. Her parents' arranged marriage had been riddled with problems, the least of which was their father's seeming inability to keep his fly zipped. And because of it her mother, despite all the money and power, had been a lonely, incomplete, miserable woman.

As far as Sophie was concerned, life was too short to spend it with a spouse she could only barely tolerate. She would rather be alone.

"So I'm guessing you didn't," she said. "Learn to love her, I mean."

"It would have been tough, seeing as how I was in love with someone else."

That admission nearly floored her, because she suspected the someone else he was referring to was her. She glanced up at him and could see from the look in his eyes, the way they cut through her, that she was. It was both disturbing and a little exciting to know that a man had loved her so much no other woman could make him happy. It also made her feel guilty, as though she had ruined his life somehow. Which was ridiculous. She hadn't forced him to marry a woman he didn't love. Just like her, he'd had choices. Any mistakes he'd made were his own.

So why wasn't that much of a consolation?

"But," he continued, "she didn't love me, either. So I guess you could say we were even. She was just in it for the name. And society rank. Beyond that, she had few real ambitions." He tucked his hands into the pockets of his slacks. "Why is it that you never married?"

"I suppose I never met a man I would want to marry."

He laughed and shook his head.

"You find that amusing?"

"In fact, I do. You claimed that you wanted to marry me. Or is that your M.O.? Seduce men, make them believe you want to marry them, then dump them with no explanation." He sounded more curious than angry, but there was an undeniable undercurrent of tension in his voice.

"It wasn't like that, Alex."

He laughed, a sharp and ironic sound. "It was exactly like that."

She shook her head. "What difference does it make now?"

"Just tell me this much—did you care at all, or were you just bored?"

"Of course I cared," she said softly. She had been weak, unable to stand up for herself. For their love. It's not something she was proud of, but there was no changing the past, and rehashing it all now wasn't going to solve anything. "I did what I had to."

That should have been the end of it, but Alex wouldn't let it drop. "So what that means is your parents disapproved, and you didn't have the guts to fight for us. Or maybe you just didn't care."

"I did care, but it's...*complicated.*"

"I'm a marginally intelligent man, Princess. Why don't you try explaining it to me?"

Nothing good would come from this, but maybe after all this time he deserved the truth. "When my parents found out about our plans to elope, they were against it, of course. But I told them I loved you, and I was going to marry you, and there was nothing they could do to stop me."

"At which point they forced you to break it off?"

She shook her head. "They started...*planning*."

He looked confused. "Planning what?"

"Our life together, Alex."

"Are you saying that they approved? That they were going to let us get married?"

She bit her lip and nodded, and she could see he was clearly confused.

"I don't understand. If they were okay with it, why did you stop taking my calls? Answering my letters?"

"I wanted to escape, Alex. I wanted...*freedom.* To live my life and make my own decisions. And there I was, right back in the very situation I was trying to avoid. My parents controlling my every move."

He digested that for a moment, then said in a very calm voice, "So what you're saying is you didn't really love me. You were just using me. You needed a ticket out, and I was convenient."

She shook her head. "No, I didn't mean it to sound like that. I loved you."

"As long as I served some sort of purpose," he said. She could see that he was angry. Angry and hurt.

"No! Letting go of you was the hardest thing I've ever done. But I had to. You had so many dreams. So many plans. You would have had to give them all up. By letting you go, I was giving you a chance to live your life."

"But that's a decision I should have made for myself."

"You would have had no idea what you were getting yourself into. Eventually you would have hated me for it, and I just couldn't bear the thought of that."

"And if you could go back and do it over?" he asked.

Had it not been for Alex, she wouldn't have known how true love, true passion and yearning felt. She may have even married the man her parents had chosen for her and spent her life lonely and miserable. Simply because that was the way things were done. In a way, Alex had saved her life.

He reached up, brushed his fingers softly against her cheek. The gesture was so sweet and tender, she wanted to cry. And she wanted to kiss him again. She wanted to feel him hold her. But Phillip's words about business and what was proper ran like a ticker tape through her head.

She turned away. "Please, Alex. Don't."

A strong breeze whipped through the gardens, chilling her to the bone. She rubbed her arms, realized how late it was getting. The sun had dipped below the trees and the outdoor lights had switched on. "It's getting dark. We should get back inside."

He shook his head, looking so…disappointed. But he let it drop.

She started in the direction of the door, but Alex just stood there. "Aren't you coming?"

"I'd like to walk for a little while longer. I'll find my way back inside."

She nodded. "I'll see you in the morning."

"What time does the tour begin?"

"Why don't we meet in the foyer at nine? Dress casually."

"Fine. I'll see you then."

Alex watched Sophie walk away, until she was swallowed up into the night, then he turned and walked in the opposite direction down the path.

Just when he thought he couldn't resent her more, she proved him wrong. He didn't buy her sob story about breaking it off for him. Sophie did things with only one person in mind. Herself.

Which made his recent plan all the more satisfying. Things were going exactly as he'd intended, and though he wasn't one to gloat, he had to admit he'd given an Oscar-worthy performance. Although it hadn't all been an act.

What he'd told her was true. He hadn't spent time with his family in ages—not since before the divorce. His mother and sister had been disappointed that he hadn't been willing to try to work things out with his wife. God only knows what Cynthia, his ex, had told them. And even if they knew about her affair, it might not have made a difference. Like most women, they stuck together.

That was one thing he'd liked about Sophie. she'd been autonomous. She claimed that most women were intimidated by her title, and those who weren't usually had some sort of agenda.

But these days he had issues with the entire female gender. And he supposed that Sophie was simply a convenient target.

She was playing right into his hand, making this almost too easy, and tomorrow the real fun would begin. And he knew without a doubt now that she deserved everything he could dish out.

Four

Alex was waiting in the foyer for her the following morning at nine sharp, just as they had agreed, and Sophie felt caught in a tug-of-war between anticipation and disappointment. So much for her silent prayer that he would be called away on business or some pressing personal matter in the wee hours of the night. It looked as though, for today at least, she was stuck with him.

But heavens, he was one attractive-looking inconvenience. He wore casual, charcoal gray slacks and a black, silk button-up shirt with the sleeves rolled to the elbows. The top two buttons were unfastened at the neck and she could see just a hint of his chest. Was it still smooth and well-defined? Would his skin still feel warm and solid under her palms?

She mentally shook away the thought. She didn't *want* to know.

"Did you sleep well?" she asked, just to be polite.

"Best sleep I've had in months," he said, and he did in fact look well-rested and chipper. She on the other hand had slept fitfully, and hopefully didn't look half as groggy and out of sorts as she felt.

"I seem to recall the last night I spent in that bed, I barely slept at all," he said, and that twinkle was back in his eye. "Of course, I had company."

She recalled that, as well. In painfully crisp detail. The way he touched her, the feel of his hands on her. And when they *had* slept, their naked bodies lay closely entwined. Arms and legs tangled in a lover's embrace. The memory made her head feel light and her skin tingle.

Is that the way it would be? Two weeks of him turning everything she said into a sexual innuendo? Well, she wouldn't give him the satisfaction of a reaction.

She fixed a bored look on her face. "It was so long ago, I guess I'd forgotten."

He just grinned, as though he could see right through her facade.

"Are you ready to go?" she asked.

The weight of his gaze burned into her skin like a hot flame. "I was born ready, Princess."

Bugger. Did he have to keep doing that? Toying with her? At this rate, it was going to be an exhausting and tedious day.

She led him through the palace to the back entrance, where the car waited. Her bodyguard held the door while they got in, then slipped into the front seat with the driver.

"What's on the schedule for today?" Alex asked as the car pulled down the driveway.

"First a tour of the Royal Inn. Some parts of the hotel are still under construction, but the majority of the renovations have already been completed. We'll have lunch in the hotel restaurant, then continue on to a tour of the area surrounding the hotel. Then we're back at the palace for dinner."

"And tomorrow?"

"A tour of the natural history museum and the science center, then if there's time, a drive up the coast."

"I don't suppose you scheduled any time to just kick back and relax in the next fourteen days."

"You and Phillip tee off at 7:00 a.m. Wednesday morning, and Thursday, Phillip plans to take you to the hunting cabin on the other side of the island for target practice. Saturday, you'll spend the day with Phillip and Hannah on the yacht."

"And my nights?" he asked, a spark of something warm and feral gleaming in his eyes.

Oh, please. Could he be any *less* subtle?

She spared him a polite smile. "Oh, I'm sure you'll figure out a way to amuse yourself."

Rather than be insulted, he laughed. "Phillip mentioned something about a black-tie charity event."

"That would be Friday night."

"You'll be there, too?"

"Of course."

"Then plan to save a dance for me."

She nodded politely, thinking, when hell froze over.

He leaned back and folded one leg over the other. "So, Princess, what is it that you normally do?"

"What do you mean?"

"I mean, if you weren't here with me, where would you be?"

She shrugged. "This *is* what I do. I'm a goodwill ambassador."

"So, you cart people around the island?"

"Among other things. I also attend and host charity functions, plan any parties or dinners. Basically, any and all public relations."

He nodded slowly. "Sounds…exciting."

She didn't miss the less-than-subtle sarcasm. Who was he to pass judgment on her? He was making it very difficult for her to be diplomatic. And she couldn't help but suspect that was exactly his intention.

And she refused to give him the satisfaction. "You disapprove?" she asked. Casually, as though it didn't matter either way.

"I guess I just imagined you doing something… *bigger.* Ten years ago, you had vast aspirations."

Normally she would be the first to admit her duties left much to be desired, but to Alex she found herself defending her position. Her composure slipping. "What I do is both important and necessary. And it's not nearly as small as you like to believe."

Rather than look offended, he grinned. "I know that, Sophie. I just wondered if you did."

What?

For the first time since…well…*ever,* someone had stunned her into total silence.

But it didn't take her long to recover.

"What the hell was that for?" she asked, then immediately regretted her sharp tone. What was wrong with her? It wasn't at all like her to let a man under her skin this way.

Of course, no man, or woman, for that matter, dared to speak to her so frankly. In an odd sense, it was almost…refreshing. A relief even to be in the presence of someone outside the family who didn't cater to her every whim.

"I get the distinct impression that you don't know how important you are," Alex said. "Do you know that Phillip has more than once referred to you as the glue that holds the family together."

And here she'd been under the impression Phillip considered her a nuisance. But what surprised her most wasn't that Phillip had those feelings, but that he'd actually voiced them.

"Well," she said, "he certainly has an interesting way of showing it."

"Brothers usually do. Particularly *older* brothers. Just ask my baby sister. More than once she's accused me of sticking my nose in where it doesn't belong. But we do it out of love. Honestly."

She found herself smiling, and immediately wiped

the expression from her face. This was all wrong. He was breaking down her defenses, getting under her skin. Inside her head.

She turned from him and gazed out the window, at the passing landscape. They were leaving the rural setting and entering the outskirts of the city.

"Something wrong?" he asked.

"No, I just…I don't want to talk about this. It isn't proper."

"Okay. What do you want to talk about?"

Nothing. She just wanted to sit quietly and brood. But those would not be the actions of a good hostess. She was supposed to be composed and polite, and at times even cheerful depending on the guest. She was like a chameleon, becoming whoever the situation required. But with Alex she wasn't sure *who* she was supposed to be.

Thank heavens they only had another few minutes before they reached the hotel. Already she could see snippets of deep blue ocean between the buildings dotting the shore line. Located in the Irish Sea, between England, Scotland, Ireland and Wales, their island was a small one, but that was its charm. Two hundred and twenty-seven square miles of pure bliss.

"I'd forgotten how beautiful the bay is," Alex said, gazing out the window. "A true paradise."

Finally, a topic of conversation that didn't revolve around her personal life. How refreshing. "We like to think so," she said.

"It's been built up quite a bit since I was last here, hasn't it?"

"The bay area has, but more than forty percent of the island is devoted to national parks and nature conservation."

"Phillip told me that tourism has nearly doubled in the past few years."

"It has." And it was no coincidence the changes began to happen after their father died, and Phillip had taken over, although unofficially at first because their mother was still the reigning queen. But unbeknownst to everyone, including her children, she had been hiding the fact that she was ill.

As a brother Phillip may have been a complete pain in the behind, but he was one hell of a fine leader. And it occurred to her that she'd never told him that. Or how proud she was of him.

"Our economy is thriving and property values are at an all-time high," she said.

"And the cost of living?"

"Higher on the coast, of course, but fairly reasonable inland."

"Decent tax incentives for local business owners?"

"Of course. Why do you ask?"

He shrugged. "Just curious."

He wasn't actually thinking of relocating there, was he? He did mention something about taking his company international. But would he go so far as to open an office here? And would that mean she would be seeing a lot more of him?

She honestly wasn't sure how she felt about that. It shouldn't have mattered at all. He was nothing to her now. At least, that's what she wanted to believe. And there was no point making assumptions.

"There it is," she told him gesturing out the window on her side as the hotel came into view, towering like a grand sentinel over the surrounding buildings.

He leaned over to see out her window, his body so close to hers she could feel heat emanating from him, smell the subtle yet familiar scent of his aftershave. And it took all of her restraint not to tense and shift away. And even more willpower not to reach out and touch him. Press her hand to his smooth jaw line. Bury her nose in the crook of his neck and breathe him in, the way she used to.

Instead she sat stock-still, hoping he couldn't feel the tension rolling off her like a turbulent ocean.

"I've seen photos," he said. "But they really don't do it justice, do they?"

"You can't truly appreciate it until you see it with your own eyes." The car pulled into the driveway at the hotel, and Sophie watched Alex's face. This was her favorite part of the tour. Watching the expressions of guests the first time they laid eyes on the structure and the scenic view. Set on the coast, mere steps from a pristine stretch of private beach, it was indeed like paradise. And she could see that Alex was genuinely impressed.

He finally sat back, and she felt as though she could breathe for the first time in minutes.

"The architecture is classic, but with the perfect balance of modern elements," he said. "I'm envious. I wish I had designed it."

"We were fortunate to find such a beautiful pre-existing building in the ideal location. Although renovations on the decor were extensive." She leaned forward and told her driver, "Take us to the service entrance in the back." She turned to Alex. "From there you can see the Houghton, and the land for the fitness center and spa."

The car pulled around the back and parked just outside the service door. As they climbed out, Alex slipped on a pair of Oakley sunglasses and followed her across the lot to the crumbling stone wall delineating their property from the Houghtons'. He moved with the grace and confidence of a man who knew exactly how good he looked and embraced it, without the vibe of arrogance she found common in men so physically appealing.

He seemed very comfortable in his own skin. But he always had.

"As you can see, we have a lot to work with as far as location," she said. "This was one of the first resort hotels to be built here. The Houghtons have owned this land for generations. Their ancestors can be traced back almost as far as the royal family."

He nodded, surveying the land, and she could practically see his mind working. He took off his sunglasses, shading his eyes from the sun with one hand as he gazed up at the structure that would soon be bulldozed to the ground. “It is a beautiful building. In the past few years, more than half of my business involves restoration, and if the Houghtons had taken better care of it, the structure might have been salvageable. But in its present condition…” He shook his head, a look of genuine regret on his face. “It’s just not a cost-effective option.”

“For many years now local businesses with qualifying historical buildings in the bay area have been offered grants to participate in a rejuvenation project. Unfortunately the Houghtons never applied.”

“I guess you can’t help people who don’t want to be helped.” He slipped his sunglasses back on and turned to her. “Why don’t we head inside the Royal Inn.”

“Of course.” They walked to the back service entrance that led to the main kitchen. Although breakfast was over, and lunch still a few hours away, it was bustling with activity and teeming with delicious scents.

“Nice,” Alex said. “Very modern.”

“Only the best.”

“Phillip tells me you’re responsible for the kitchen renovations.”

“Partially, yes.”

“He also said that you’re an accomplished chef.”

Did he also mention that he disapproved? She wouldn’t be at all surprised. “It’s my one true passion. I studied in France.”

“I remember that you used to be very passionate,” he said, with that sizzling grin. Why was he so intent on trying to knock her off base? "That must have been after I met you. Culinary school, I mean."

She nodded. Although not long after. One more thing she could thank him for, in a roundabout way.

"I never would have imagined that your parents would just let you leave."

Normally they wouldn't have. But for the first time in her life, she'd had leverage. "Let's just say we bartered a deal."

"That must have been some deal."

For all the good it did her. After she came home, it was back to her royal duties. She should have known her parents would never let her have an actual career. And leave it to Phillip, despite his animosity toward their parents, to cling to the same archaic ideas.

"It's always been my dream to own a restaurant and run the kitchen." She looked around, at the interior that was almost solely her design, the appliances she had ordered. The menu she herself had supplied.

She may never get the opportunity to use it, but this was *her* kitchen. "I guess this is the closest I'll ever get."

Someone dropped a pan in the kitchen, and at the loud clang that vibrated through the room, her bodyguard was instantly at her side. She waved him away, and he immediately backed off.

Alex looked as apprehensive as he was impressed. "How many bodyguards normally escort you?"

"Depending on the occasion, members of the royal family never leave the palace without at least one armed escort. Except Ethan, but he's the only exception." She nodded toward the bodyguard who now trailed them by a watchful ten paces. "And Maurice is one of our most lethal. Isn't that right, Maurice?"

Maurice cracked just the hint of a dangerous-looking grin.

"You don't find it unnerving to have someone constantly following you?" Alex asked.

"I'm so used to it, I barely notice him there. And it's a necessity."

"Have there been threats against you?"

She was surprised to see a look of genuine concern on his face. Did he honestly still care about her after all these years?

"Not me personally," she assured him. "Or Phillip. But you can never be too careful. There was an attempted assassination on our father's father many years ago. And our father, King Frederick, had his share of disgruntled citizens. He was a very arrogant and, I'm sorry to say, self-serving leader."

Sadly, her father's methods and ideals had turned Sophie against the entire idea of a monarchy. Only since Phillip had taken over had her feelings begun to change, and it had been a gradual transformation.

"Let's move on," she said, gesturing to the kitchen door.

They walked through the service hallway out into the main wing, and while her appearances in public often caused something of a spectacle, as they toured the lobby with it's elegant decor and grand water display, she noticed that many eyes were instead focused on Alex. And why wouldn't they be? He was the type of man that other men viewed with envy and women eyed with appreciation. She wasn't the jealous type, but under different circumstances…

Circumstances that would never happen in a million years, she reminded herself.

Five

After a walkthrough of the guest rooms and facilities, and lunch at *Les Régals du Rois,* the hotel's newly acclaimed French restaurant, Alex was thoroughly impressed by the Royal Inn. It was both elegant and elite, but tailored to the common traveler, as well as the privileged, businesspeople and vacationers alike.

In terms of size, this project wasn't what he would consider significant; but in terms of notoriety, he'd hit pay dirt.

"So, what do you think of our hotel?" Sophie asked, when they were in the car and on their way back to the palace.

"I think the royal family has one hell of a sound investment."

She actually smiled. And here he'd been wondering if she'd forgotten how. And it was evident that she was quite proud of what the royal family had accomplished.

"I'm no hotel expert, but there is one thing I would consider," he said.

"Yes, please." She sat forward, looking genuinely interested. "You probably know far more than I do."

Her reaction made him smile. The women in his life, especially lately, seemed to think they knew everything, it was refreshing to meet one who wasn't afraid to admit her weaknesses.

"In researching the bay area, I noticed that there are no hotels equipped to handle a conference of any significant size. You may want to look into expanding your facilities."

"And you think that would bring more business?"

"It's an untapped market, so I think it would be worth looking into."

"I'll mention it to Phillip and Ethan."

Finally, he'd said something that hadn't elicited a frown or a disapproving look. But when it came to business, he didn't mess around. But now maybe it was time to shake things up a bit.

"So, what are we doing next?" he asked. "A ride up the coast?"

"That will have to wait. Phillip set aside time this afternoon so you and he can catch up."

Although he looked forward to spending time with his friend, Alex couldn't deny feeling a little disappointed. He'd made progress with Sophie today, managed to chip away at her resolve. She wasn't so tense around him. So quick to distrust. At this rate, in a few days he would have her right where he wanted her.

But there was no rush, he reminded himself. He had two weeks. Plenty of time to get what he wanted. And honestly, this vacation was exactly what he needed. He couldn't recall the last time he'd felt so relaxed, a morning when he woke not dreading the day.

"Thanks for taking the time to shuttle me around," he told Sophie.

She shrugged. "It's what I do."

"And you do it well, Your Highness."

Her brow furrowed and she studied him for several seconds, then she shook her head.

"What?" he asked.

"Nothing."

"It's obviously not nothing," he said, playing dumb. "Why did you look at me like that?"

"Just drop it."

"You need to learn how to take a compliment, Princess."

Her jaw tensed almost imperceptibly and there was an edge to her tone. "Maybe you should word your compliments so they're not so…"

"So what?"

"Suggestive."

He laughed. "Telling you that you're good at your job? How is that suggestive?"

He could see her struggling with her composure. She wanted to explode, but he knew she wouldn't give him the satisfaction. What she didn't realize is that he felt more satisfaction watching her struggle than if she'd blown up in his face.

"Okay," he admitted. "Maybe it was a little suggestive, but, Princess, you are awfully fun to tease. I take it you don't get that very often."

"No, I don't"

He grinned. "Well, you'll just have to get used to it, I guess."

She made a quiet huffing noise. "It's not as if I have a choice."

She had no idea. "You shouldn't take life so seriously, Your Highness."

Her expression darkened. "You know nothing about me, Alex."

He knew she was spoiled and arrogant. And let's not forget entitled. And although she was obviously used to getting her way, she had no idea who she was up against.

And he was having far too much fun breaking her spirit.

It was barely three in the afternoon, but when Sophie returned to her residence, she felt as though she had just endured one of the longest days of her life.

She didn't blame Alex for feeling bitter about their past, but the man was sending so many mixed signals that she was getting whiplash.

The car dropped her at her front door, and Wilson met her in the vestibule.

"Prince Ethan rang while you were gone, Miss. He asked that you contact him immediately upon your return home. He said it's urgent."

She sighed quietly. The last thing she needed was more undue drama in her day, but Ethan wasn't one to exaggerate. If he said it was important, it most likely was.

"Thank you, Wilson. I'll ring him right now."

Using the phone in the study, she dialed his number and he answered on the first ring.

"Could I come by and speak with you?" he asked, and he did indeed sound rattled. Which wasn't at all like him.

Her first thought was that Lizzy had taken a turn for the worse.

"Of course. Is something wrong?"

"Not exactly. I'm at the palace, so I'll be there in a few minutes."

She barely had time to use the powder room and freshen her makeup before she heard the throaty growl of his engine out front, then the sound of the bell announcing his presence.

Rather than wait for Wilson, she opened the door herself. "That was quick."

He tagged her with a quick peck on the cheek on his way in. In his hand he clutched a manila envelope. "I could use a drink."

Although Ethan was one of the most laid-back

men she'd ever known, he was visibly agitated. "Well then, let's go to the study," she said.

He followed her there and watched while she poured him two fingers of her best scotch straight up, then poured herself a glass of white wine.

She handed him his drink. "What's so urgent that it couldn't wait?"

He took a long swallow, then asked, "Does the name Richard Thornsby ring a bell?"

"If you're referring to the Richard Thornsby who was prime minister of Morgan Isle when our father's reign began, then yes, of course I know who he is." But the question was, why did Ethan know? Thornsby had been dead for years. And what did it matter?

"The way I understand it, he and our father didn't exactly see eye to eye," Ethan said.

"That's putting it mildly. They were mortal enemies."

"Did he ever tell you why?"

"I would never dare ask. We weren't even permitted to so much as utter his name in the palace. Even after his death he was never mentioned. I just assumed it was because they had vast differences of opinion."

"I read that our father had him ousted from his position, which more or less ruined him politically."

"King Frederick was ruthless. He had no tolerance for anyone who didn't see things his way." She couldn't help wondering where he was going with this. "Why are you suddenly so interested in our father's political dealings?"

"I'm getting to that." He took another swallow of his drink and set the empty glass down on the table. "Thornsby and his wife were killed a couple of years later."

"Yes. A car accident."

"But there was one survivor of the crash."

"That's right. Their ten-year-old daughter. I believe her name is Melissa."

"It is. Melissa Angelica Thornsby. When her parents died, she was sent to live with relatives in the States."

"If you say so. Like I told you, their names weren't spoken in our home. And I mean, *never.*"

"I think I know why. And it has nothing to do with political diversity."

"I'm not following you." And the curiosity of what could possibly be in the envelope was gnawing away at her patience.

"I think their differences were more...*personal* in nature."

All this ambiguity was getting on her nerves. "Ethan, would you please just say what you have to say?"

"Our father's reputation as a womanizer is no secret, so it stands to reason that there could be more of us out there."

"Us?"

"Royal heirs. Illegitimate ones, like me. With Phillip's permission I've been looking into it. Yesterday I was in the attic going through our father's things and I found these." He finally handed her the envelope.

She opened it up and dumped the contents out on the table. It was mostly magazine articles and newspaper clippings. And it didn't take long to determine their theme. They were all about Thornsby's daughter, Melissa. "I don't get it."

"Think about it, Sophie. Why would our father collect a bunch of articles about the daughter of his most despised rival?"

He couldn't possibly mean what she thought he meant. "Ethan, that's ridiculous."

He picked out one of the articles that had a snapshot of Melissa. "Look at her, Sophie. The dark hair, the shape of her face."

She couldn't deny there were striking similarities. "You honestly think she's our sister?"

"I think it's a definite possibility."

If their father had an affair with the Prime Minister's wife, that would certainly explain their ill will toward each other. And sadly, given their father's reputation, it was not only very possible, but altogether likely.

"And if she is family?" Sophie asked.

"If she is, we might have a huge problem."

"Well, yes, more scandal that the royal family really doesn't need."

"It's worse than that."

"How much worse?"

"She was born the same year as Phillip. One month *before* him. And as I'm sure you well know that the king's firstborn, male or female, inherits the crown."

Oh, yeah, that was pretty bad.

Sophie's heart fisted into a knot. "So if she is our sister, then she would be the rightful leader. Not Phillip."

"It seems that way."

She couldn't even imagine what that would do to Phillip, or what it would mean for their country. "Does Phillip know?"

Ethan shook his head. "I wanted to talk to you first, get your take on this."

Her first instinct was to burn what proof Ethan had already gathered and sweep the charred remains under the nearest rug. But what if it was true and Melissa Thornsby really was their sister? Had Sophie denied Ethan as her brother, she would have lost out on what had become one of her closest and dearest relationships. How could they deny a member of their family?

But there was so much at stake.

"So, do we tell Phillip?" Ethan asked.

"I think for now we should keep this quiet and not say anything to Phillip until we have some proof. There's no reason to upset him over nothing."

"I'd like to talk with Charles and ask him to find out what he can about her."

"I think that's a good idea. We can trust him to be discreet. We should also have him look into what can be done if she *is* an heir and decides she wants to question Phillip's reign."

"If Phillip finds out that we went behind his back on this, he'll be furious."

"When the time comes, I'll deal with Phillip. You just worry about finding out if she's an heir."

"This could be a real mess, Sophie. Especially if she harbors any ill will against the royal family."

Which was entirely possible. "We'll worry about that when we know a bit more about who she is. If she is the rightful heir, with any luck she'll have no interest in the crown."

She wanted to believe that, but lately, it seemed as though nothing was ever that simple.

Pleading a headache, which, after her conversation with Ethan was the wholehearted truth, Sophie was spared dinner that night with their "guest." Unfortunately she had no choice but to spend the entire next day with Alex, touring the science center and natural history museum. And even though this was usually her favorite part of any tour, she had so many other things on her mind that she was distracted. She found herself rushing through the exhibits. Or trying to at least. Alex seemed content to take his time. She'd seen snails in the garden move faster.

And why did he have to stand so close all the time? It seemed he was always right there. *Touching* her. Not any kind of overt groping. Even he was more subtle than that. Just a brush of his arm or the bump of his shoulder. Did he have no concept of personal space?

And if it was so awful, why did her skin break out in goose bumps every time he made contact? Why did she shiver with awareness?

And God help her did he smell good. The familiar, ideal blend of his aftershave, shampoo and his unique scent. Every time he was close, she had to fight the urge to bury her face against his neck and breathe him in. How could she loathe someone so, yet lust after him like a hormonally challenged adolescent?

All day he seemed intent on testing her patience, and it was working. She felt as if she were being pulled in ten different directions at once.

By the time they reached the palace gate, she was so edgy and out of sorts that her left eye had begun to twitch. She asked the driver to please drop her at home first, and when they pulled up to her residence, she was so desperate to be free of the cloying confines of the backseat that she had to sit on her hands to keep herself from clawing the car door open, and instead waited for her bodyguard.

"Well," she said, turning to Alex. "It was a pleasant day. I'll see you Thursday."

She was almost home free, with one foot out the door, when Alex asked, "Aren't you going to invite me in for a drink?"

She closed her eyes and sighed quietly. *Don't let him see you squirm.*

The most disturbing thing about his request is that she actually wanted him to come in, which was precisely why she couldn't allow it.

She turned to him. "Today isn't convenient."

He studied her for a moment, then smiled and said, "Oh, I get it."

Every fiber of her being was screaming that he was baiting her. Despite that, she couldn't stop herself from saying, "You get what?"

"I see the way you react when I'm around. The way you look at me, the way you shudder when we touch."

Shudder? Shiver a little, maybe, and not *every* time.

But to deny it would only give him exactly what he wanted. An argument.

Gathering the last strands of her patience, she fixed a bored look on her face. "And your point is…?"

"Simple. You want me, and you don't trust yourself to be alone with me."

He was clever. No matter what she did now, invite him in or tell him to get lost, she would be giving Alex what he wanted. A reaction. And whether he actually believed that or was just baiting her, she had the uneasy suspicion that he might be right. She was still attracted to Alex on a deep, visceral level. If he kissed her again, against her will or not, she was afraid this time she might not stop him.

She sat there with one foot still in the car and the other on the driveway, unsure of what to do.

"Well," he asked, looking more amused than impatient.

"There's no winning this one, is there?" she said. "I'm damned if I do and damned if I don't."

"You seem to believe that I have some evil ulterior motives, Your Highness. But has it occurred to you that maybe I'd just like a little time to get to know you? So you could maybe get to know me? I'm not a bad guy. Honestly."

She couldn't decide which was worse. Men with ulterior motives she could handle. They were refreshingly predictable and easy to deconstruct. It was the sincere ones she had trouble with.

Probably because they were such a rare anomaly.

"We just spent two days together," she reminded him. "How much time do you need?"

"Maybe I'd like a little time *without* the bodyguard hanging on our every word."

There lies the problem, she mused. She *needed* her bodyguard around hanging on their every word. And not just to protect her from Alex. That would be too easy.

She needed someone to protect her from herself.

Six

For the first time since he'd arrived, Alex saw a brief but very real flash of vulnerability in Sophie's face. And he almost felt guilty for manipulating her.

Almost.

He hadn't gotten this far in life by being soft. Unfortunately, neither had she. Which is why he figured a few drinks would probably take the edge off. Loosen her up a little.

But he had the distinct feeling he was one step away from pushing too far, so he tried a different angle. The pity card. When all else failed, women could never resist a man who shared his feelings.

"I happen to know for a fact that Phillip is away

today," he told her. "And the truth is, I don't feel like spending the rest of the afternoon alone."

He could see the arrow hit its mark. Her eyes warmed and the hard edges of her expression softened almost imperceptibly.

She considered that for a moment, then sighed quietly, and he knew he had her.

"I had planned to take a walk on the grounds," she finally said. "You could join me, I suppose. But then afterward I really have things to do."

He should have known she would suggest a compromise. That way she was giving in without actually relinquishing control.

She was good, no doubt about it. But he was better.

He grinned and said, "You've got yourself a deal, Princess."

She got out of the car and he climbed out behind her. The sun was high in the cloudless blue, its rays relentlessly intense. It seemed like a better day to lay around in the shade than take a walk, but he wasn't in any position to argue.

The bodyguard looked from Alex to Sophie and asked, "Will you be needing me, Your Highness?"

What did he think Alex was going to do? Kidnap her? Drag her off the grounds on foot?

He looked over at Sophie, and when he saw her expression, thought for a second that she just might tell him to join them. But after a slight pause she shook her head and said, "You can go."

Alex followed her to the door, mesmerized by

the liquid grace that propelled her forward. The hypnotizing sway of her hips. She was wearing one of those sheer, gauzy numbers that conformed to her figure. Hugged her in all the right places. The sharp tug of arousal low in his gut was undeniable and intense.

They reached the threshold and the door swung open.

"Miss," Wilson said, bowing his head as they stepped inside. Alex could swear the man shot him a disapproving look. Her staff was obviously protective of her, and he had the feeling their concern was as much personal as it was professional. Which had him wondering, if she was as spoiled and manipulative as she used to be, why would they hold her in such high regard?

Or maybe she reserved that behavior for her lovers.

"Wilson, will you show our guest into the study and pour him a drink?"

"Of course," Wilson said.

She turned to Alex. "I just need to change. I'll only be a minute or two."

"Take your time," he said, watching her climb the steps, the way she seemed to almost float, as light as air. Damn she was sexy, and he was looking forward to getting his hands on her again, to see just how much she'd changed over the past ten years.

"Mr. Rutledge," Wilson said with a distinct note of disapproval in his voice. And when Alex turned to him, he gestured toward the study door. "After you."

When they were in the study Wilson asked, "What can I get you, sir?"

"Mineral water with lemon, if it's not too much trouble."

Wilson crossed the room to the bar, and Alex made himself comfortable on the sofa. "Have you worked for Princess Sophie very long?" he asked.

"I've been with the royal family for more than forty years."

"That's a long time."

"Yes, sir."

"You take care of Sophie."

"Yes, sir, I do. And it's not a task I take lightly."

Alex couldn't escape the feeling that he was being judged not by an employee, but a father considering the motives of a potential son-in-law.

And because Alex had always been one to face his adversaries head-on, he asked very bluntly. "You don't trust me, do you?"

Wilson walked over to the couch and handed him his drink. "I've found, sir, that paranoia is often the result when one has something to hide."

Oh, ouch. A direct hit. Were he a weaker man, he might have retreated. And while some considered him reckless for it, Jonah in particular, he never backed down from a challenge. Even when the odds weren't necessarily in his favor. "And what is it that you think I'm hiding?"

"I couldn't say, but it's quite obvious you have some sort of agenda."

"And you feel the need to protect her from me?"

Wilson smiled and there was an undeniable twinkle of amusement in his eyes. "Oh, no, sir. Her Highness doesn't need protecting. Not from you or anyone else. And if you believe she does, that will be your downfall."

They would just see about that, wouldn't they?

Before he could manufacture a snappy comeback, Sophie appeared in the doorway. She had changed into jogging shorts, a tank top and athletic shoes, and her hair was pulled back in a ponytail.

And she still managed to look superior and elegant.

"Heading to the gym?" Alex asked.

"Going on a walk," she said. "I walk briskly for an hour every day."

"I was thinking more along the lines of a casual stroll."

She shrugged. "So don't go with me."

It was pushing eighty-five degrees outside, and dressed the way he was, he risked heat stroke. Not to mention ruining his four-hundred-dollar Brazilian leather loafers. But he couldn't exactly back out now, could he? And he didn't bother to ask for time to change, since he already knew what the answer would be.

Wilson cleared his throat. "If there's nothing else you need, Your Highness, I should check on dinner."

"Of course," Sophie said, dismissing him with a nod and a smile.

On his way out, Wilson wore a polite smile, but

as he glanced Alex's way, his eyes clearly said, *I told you so.*

Sophie stepped behind the bar and grabbed two bottles of water from the refrigerator, then looked Alex up and down, said, "I don't think one is going to cut it," and grabbed one more.

She was probably right.

"Are you ready?" she asked.

At this point he didn't have much choice. And damned if Wilson wasn't right. He had underestimated her.

But that wasn't a mistake he would be making again.

Despite the heat, and his inappropriate clothing, Sophie had to admit that Alex did a pretty good job keeping up with her. Not that he wasn't feeling the heat. Sweat poured from his face and soaked the back of his silk shirt. He had already guzzled one bottle of water and was a third of the way through his second.

That's what he got for messing with her. As she'd heard Wilson say, he shouldn't underestimate her. He was clever, but she had a few tricks up her sleeve, too.

She led him along the lawn paths, even though typically, on a day as hot as this one, she would have taken refuge on the paths in the woods under the dense canopy of leaves. Someone up there must have been looking out for him though, because a line of dark clouds rolled in shortly after they began walking, dampening the sun's relentless afternoon glare.

"Looks like rain," he said, gazing up at the sky.

Then he looked back at her residence, a good quarter mile from their current location. "Maybe we should head back."

Nice try. "Afraid you'll melt?"

"I'm already melting," he said wryly. "I just don't want to get stuck out here during a storm."

"This is the dry season. It hardly ever rains. The clouds will most likely blow right over us." Although they did look rather dark and ominous and the wind was picking up.

"It doesn't look like it's going to roll over us," he pressed.

She rolled her eyes. "Don't be such a baby."

"I don't know about you, but I don't relish the idea of getting struck by lightning."

"Even if it does rain, these storms blow over quickly. I'm sure we're perfectly safe." Just in case, she altered her direction so they were walking in the direction of the woods.

They barely made it another ten paces when a fat, cold drop of rain landed on her cheek. Then another splashed on her forearm.

"See," Alex said, holding a hand out to catch a drop in his palm. "Those are raindrops."

"A little rain isn't going to kill us. In fact, you look as if you could use some cooling off."

He opened his mouth to reply just as a bolt of lightning streaked across the sky and a deafening crack of thunder drowned out whatever sarcastic snipe he'd been about to fling her way.

She screeched in surprise and they both instinctively ducked. In the next instant, the heavens seemed to open like a floodgate and rain came down in a waterfall. Big, fat, cold drops, soaking her to the skin in a matter of seconds.

"Head for the woods!" she yelled, and they both took off running in that direction. Probably not the best place to be in a thunderstorm, but if they didn't find cover, they risked drowning.

In the thirty seconds it took to reach the marginal cover of the trees, she felt, and probably looked, like a drowned rat.

"I'm officially cooled off," he said, slicking back his hair. It was drenched and leaking water down his face and his clothes were plastered to his body like a second skin.

And, *oh,* what a body it was. She could see every sculpted ridge of muscle in his chest and arms, his slim waist and muscular thighs. He was bigger than he'd been in college. Even more perfect, if that was possible.

Suddenly she wasn't feeling cold anymore. There was a delicious warmth building inside her that had absolutely nothing to do with the weather and everything to do with the man standing in front of her.

Fight it, Sophie.

"So much for it just *blowing over,*" Alex said.

"Yeah. Oops." She shivered and pulled the band from her drooping ponytail, twisting the rain from her hair. "You're the one who insisted on going with me."

He squeezed the excess rain from his shirt. "Yet I can't help but think you did this on purpose."

"You think I can control the weather? I'm good, Alex, but I'm not that good."

Only after the words were out, when Alex's eyes locked on hers, deep and piercing and full of lust, did she realize how that sounded. But it was too late to take it back. She wasn't even sure if she wanted to.

"That's not the way I remember it," he said, his voice husky. His eyes slipped lower, to her lips, then her throat, then lower still, and she knew without looking that her nipples were two hard points poking through the wet fabric of her sports bra and tank. She couldn't help noticing that he, too, was looking a bit chilly. On top anyway. Down below, she could swear that things were looking rather…lofty.

He lifted his eyes to hers, blue and piercing, and she practically shuddered with awareness. He took a step closer and every cell in her body went on high alert.

A drop of rain leaked out of her hair and rolled down her cheek. Alex reached up, almost absently, and wiped it away with the pad of his thumb. He might as well have brushed that thumb between her thighs because that's where the sensation seemed to settle.

She had no doubt that the end result of this situation was going to be a kiss. It was inevitable. And the only thing worse than kissing him would be letting him make the first move, allowing him to take control. So she didn't give him the chance. She grabbed the front of his shirt, curling her fingers in the sodden fabric, tugged him to her, and pressed her lips to his.

If he was surprised by her advances, it didn't take him long to collect himself. He groaned and wove a hand through her wet and tangled hair, pulled her against him. She parted her lips for him, invited him, and when his tongue touched hers, she went weak all over.

They feasted on…no, *devoured* each other. But it wasn't enough. She wanted him closer, *deeper.* She felt as though she were starving, that she'd been slowly withering away the past ten years and the only thing that could nourish her back to life was his touch. His hands on her skin. And that need seemed to cancel out whatever was left of her rational side.

She tore at the front of his shirt, wanting, no *needing,* bare skin to touch, to run her hands over. She felt buttons give way and heard the fabric tear. His skin was warm and wet and she could feel his heart hammering wildly in his chest.

Alex backed her against the nearest tree, pinning her to the rough bark with the full length of his body. Sophie gasped at the sharp sting, but it was both pain and pleasure. For the first time in God knows how long, she felt whole again, and it frightened her half to death. This was just like the first time. Passionate to the point of feeling almost desperate. A deep yearning to connect.

It was just starting to get good when he tore his

mouth from hers, his breath rasping out in harsh bursts, and said, "Listen."

Did he hear someone coming? She stopped to listen, but she didn't hear a thing other than the quiet sounds of the forest. "What?"

"It stopped raining," he said.

Yeah, so?

He eased away from her. "We should head back."

Head back? Was he *serious?*

For a moment she was too stunned to reply. He obviously wanted this just as much as she did. He'd been leading up to this for days. So why the sudden change of heart?

Then she realized exactly what was happening. This was just a game to him. He'd planned this all along. She should have known. He obviously got some kind of warped satisfaction from getting her all worked up then shooting her down.

And shame on her for falling for it. For letting him get the best of her.

And he could be damned sure it wouldn't happen again.

Seven

In the blink of an eye, Sophie's expression went from one of confusion to barely contained rage. And all Alex could do was follow her as she turned and walked purposely back in the direction they'd come, toward her house.

He'd had Sophie right where he wanted her, but when the time came to seal the deal, he couldn't go through with it. It wasn't supposed to happen this way. She wasn't supposed to make the first move. And he wasn't supposed to feel this deep sense of…something. An emotion so foreign he couldn't identify it. Something more than desire or lust. He felt…whole.

Complete.

And that was just sentimental bull. She'd caught him off guard, that was all.

Sophie was moving so fast she was practically jogging, and any second he expected her to break into full run.

"You want to slow down?" he asked, his feet squishing in shoes swimming with at least an inch of water.

She didn't answer. She just kept chugging along, and damn, she was fast. But he was faster.

He caught up and clamped a hand around her upper arm. "Slow down, Sophie."

She jerked free. "Why should I? I'm do exactly as you suggested. Heading back."

"Jesus, you're stubborn," he muttered.

She stopped so abruptly, swinging around to face him, that he nearly plowed right into her.

"I'm *stubborn,*" she ground out through clenched teeth, unleashing the full wrath of her anger.

He knew she had a temper, but damn.

He took a step back, for fear that if he got too close, she might take a swing at him. "I just want to talk to you."

"What for? You already won."

"Won what?"

"This juvenile little game you've been playing with me."

She was right. It was a game. And he should be enjoying this, basking in the glow of defeat. Instead he felt like a slime.

It would seem that the joke was on him.

He just needed a chance to regroup, to get things back on track. To shake off these feelings of guilt.

And to perform a bit of damage control.

"Do you feel better now that you've gotten your revenge?" she asked. "Do you feel vindicated?"

"Sophie, listen to yourself," he said calmly. "I kiss you and you threaten to have me arrested for assault, then you kiss me, and you get mad when I put on the brakes? And you accuse *me* of playing games?"

"You're absolutely right," she said, even though it was obvious she was just agreeing with him to shut him up. "Case closed."

He opened his mouth to argue, but she held up a hand to shush him. "I'm going home now. *Do not* follow me."

Even though he was tempted to follow her anyway, push her just a little further, instinct told him to back off. He changed direction and headed toward the palace instead.

Sophie charged into Phillip's outer office, stunning his secretary into silence before she could even try to stop her from flinging open Phillip's office door. And Phillip was there, sitting behind his desk, despite the fact that Alex said he was away this afternoon.

Another lie. No big surprise.

Phillip looked her up and down, taking in her dripping, tangled hair and soaked clothes. "What the hell happened to you?"

She held up the agenda for Alex's visit and flung

it onto his desk. "Find someone else to babysit your friend. I'm finished."

He calmly folded his hands, looking almost amused. "I could swear we already had this discussion."

"Well, we're having it *again.*"

He sat back in his chair and for a long moment only studied her. Then he shook his head. "No, you're going to do it, as planned."

She struggled to maintain an iota of control. "*No,* I'm not."

"You're sure about that?"

She parked her hands on her hips and glared at him. "Don't I *sound* sure?"

"Fine. Then from this moment forward you'll be cut out of the business. The only duties you'll have will be your royal ones."

Her mouth fell open. "Are you joking?"

"Do I look like I'm joking?"

She was so angry and frustrated that she felt like stomping her feet.

"You can see that I'm miserable. Are you *trying* to torture me?"

"What I'm trying to do is teach you that this is a business and you can't pick and choose what you will or won't do on a whim. Because what that says to me is that you cannot be counted on."

"This is different."

"*How* is it different? Give me one good reason why I should grant your request."

She couldn't tell him the real reason. And the best she could come up with was, "He makes me… uncomfortable."

One of Phillip's eyebrows rose a notch. "He's behaved inappropriately?"

Alex *had* kissed her his first day here, but to be fair, she'd been the one to make the first move today in the woods, so they were kind of even in the inappropriate-behavior department. "Not exactly."

Phillip sat up a little straighter in his chair. "If he has, friend or not, I'll fire him from the project immediately and send him back to the U.S. on the first available flight. Just say the word."

She may have been furious with Alex, but she also didn't want to come between him and Phillip. Not personally or professionally. "He hasn't done anything inappropriate. I just…I don't like him."

"So, what, he doesn't kiss your royal behind, and therefore you can't tolerate him?"

"Phillip!"

"That's what I figured." He relaxed back into his chair, a wry grin curling his mouth. "Sophie, do you think I like everyone I have to work with? That's just business. Get used to it."

She was no stranger to the concept. Had he forgotten the countless "guests" she had catered to and shuttled all over the island? They ranged from polite and friendly to odd and unusual and some who were just downright creepy. And she'd never complained. At least, not *too* much. And she always did what was expected of her. She would think that just this once he could cut her a little slack.

But then he wouldn't be Phillip if he did that.

"Fine," she said, smoothing back her knotted hair as best she could. She must have looked positively dreadful. She could have at least taken the time to change into dry clothes and run a brush through her hair. Of course, if she'd been at all rational, she never would have come to see him in the first place.

"You might want to rethink the new look," he said, amusement dancing in his eyes. He did that a lot now. Smiling, laughing. Before Hannah came into his life he was a much darker person. She was glad he was happy. She only wished he weren't so determined to make her miserable instead.

She looked down at her ensemble. "What, you don't like it?"

"Got caught in the rain during your walk?"

"How'd you guess?"

"I was on my way in from a meeting a few minutes before you barged in here, and I ran into Alex who was in pretty much the same condition."

So, Phillip *had* been away at a meeting. At least Alex hadn't lied about that. She wondered if Phillip had noticed that Alex's shirt had been suspiciously divested of its buttons. "I guess he got caught in the rain, too."

"I figured you would know that since, according to Alex, you were walking together."

She couldn't help but wonder what else Alex had told him. And rather than try to come up with a plausible explanation for her sudden memory loss, she didn't say anything at all. And he let it slide.

"So, we're in agreement?" he asked.

"We're in agreement."

"You're not going to barge in here in a day or two with the same demands."

"You won't hear another word out of me about it." And at the very least, she had tomorrow to herself. A full day to recover before having to play babysitter again.

"Good."

"I should go change."

"Please do."

"I'll see you later."

She was almost to the door when he called out to her. "By the way, I forgot to mention, I had to cancel our golf trip tomorrow morning. Urgent business. So Alex is in your capable hands for the day. With any luck I can squeeze in an evening round."

So much for her day off. Would she ever catch a break?

"Is that a problem?"

She forced a smile, when what she really felt like doing was groaning, and said, "No, no problem."

"Good. I've already told Alex, and he said he'll meet you in the foyer tomorrow morning. The usual time."

"Very well. It's short notice, but I'm sure I can come up with something for us to do."

"He said he would like a relaxing day, so I took

the liberty of suggesting a day out on the yacht. He's quite looking forward to it."

Hours stuck together on a boat. She could hardly wait. "Even better. I'll call the marina and have everything prepared."

"It's already been done."

"Good."

"Also, we're taking Alex to the country club for dinner and wondered if you could watch Frederick. Maybe until eleven or so?"

"Of course." That at least wouldn't be a hardship. She adored her nephew.

"Hannah will call and let you know what time we plan to leave."

"Anything else?" she asked.

"No, I believe that's it."

"You know, I'm proud of you, Phillip."

"I beg your pardon."

"I said, I'm proud of you."

He narrowed his eyes at her. "What do you want?"

She smiled. "Nothing at all."

He looked skeptical, as though he wasn't sure he could believe her.

"Really," she assured him. "I just wanted you to know."

"Well then…thank you."

She turned to leave, but he called to her just before she reached the door.

"You know that the things I say and do are because I care."

"I know."

"Have fun tomorrow." He turned to his computer and started tapping away at the keyboard, his less-than-subtle way to dismiss her.

But as she was closing the door behind her she glanced back and saw that he had an amused, almost quirky grin and she couldn't shake the feeling that Phillip knew more than he was letting on.

All the way back to her residence Sophie mulled over in her head how she planned to handle the rest of Alex's visit. They simply couldn't go on with the way things had been these first two days. She would be loony by week's end. There had to be some way to fix this, some sort of compromise in which she would maintain control, of course.

Despite knowing what a pest Alex could be, she was still surprised to see him sitting on her porch step when she returned to her residence. And even though the idea of another argument was utterly exhausting, leaving this unresolved to ferment and fester wasn't high on her list of fun options, either. So, rather than storm past him into the house, she took a seat next to him.

He had changed into dry clothes—and a shirt with buttons—and sat slightly hunched with his arms draped over his knees. He looked unassuming and maybe a little tired. And he was so handsome, so physically perfect in every way that a hollow ache settled in her heart.

For several minutes they sat together in silence, then he finally said, "I feel as though I owe you an apology, but I'm not really sure what I'm apologizing for."

That was probably the most honest thing he'd said since this nightmare of a week had begun. Clueless, but honest nonetheless.

They had spent a total of two days together, yet she felt that she *knew* him. And she felt she barely knew him at all. Nothing about this made any sense.

"If it's any consolation," she said. "I feel the same way."

He shot her a grin. "Then technically, our feelings should just what, cancel out each other?"

"If only life worked that way, the world would be a much simpler place."

"Amen to that."

She sighed and hugged her legs, resting her chin on her knees. "It's not my fault, you know."

He looked over at her. "What isn't your fault?"

"Your marriage. The fact that it was so bad."

"Did I say it was?"

"Not in so many words, but it's obvious you blame me. Or you're just bitter at the entire gender and I'm an easy target."

A frown furrowed the space between his brows. "I'd considered that as a definite possibility."

Again, very honest. Maybe that was the key to solving their problem. Maybe, rather than ignoring this undercurrent of tension, this unfinished business between them, it would be more productive to just lay all their cards on the table and settle this once and for all.

Easier said than done. Baring her soul had never been one of her strengths. She had been groomed since birth to hold her feelings inside. To never show weakness. And right now, she'd never felt more vulnerable in her life.

But she had to at least try.

She took a deep breath and blew it out. Here goes nothing.

"I did love you, Alex, and I wanted to marry you. But believe me when I say I did you a favor by ending it. It was too…big. Bigger than either of us was prepared for. The sacrifices we would have had to make…" She shook her head. "We just would have ended up resenting each other."

He shrugged. "I guess we'll never know."

That was just the thing. She *did* know. She'd seen it time and time again. "I'm sorry for hurting you. But I honestly felt as though I didn't have a choice."

"You did what you felt was right. I can't really fault you for that, can I? I just would have liked the opportunity to make the choice myself."

He could fault her if he wanted to. If he wanted to hold a grudge. But she hoped he wouldn't. She would like them to be able to get past this. To be friends.

"As far as my marriage goes," he said, "I'm the only one to blame. I may have been pressured by my family, but no one held a gun to my head. The truth is, I took the easy way out. Or at least, at the time it seemed easy."

In a way, she was guilty of the same thing. Ending things with Alex had been so much easier than sticking around and trying to make it work. Surely they would have had a few good years before it all fell apart. At the time she'd felt that by ending it sooner rather than later, she had been giving each of them a chance to find happiness with someone else. How could she have known neither of them would take it?

"I ended it badly," she said. "I should have called or written, given you some explanation. I was just so afraid."

"Afraid of what?"

"That if I heard your voice, I would change my mind. Or that you would talk me out of it."

"I guess you did what you had to."

"Think we'll ever get past it?"

He looked over at her, the hint of a grin tugging at the corner of his mouth. "I think it's a definite possibility."

"There's that other problem, too."

"Which problem is that?"

She hugged her legs tighter. "The sexual tension."

He shrugged. "I don't have a problem with that."

"Come on, Alex. You have to admit it's getting… *tedious.*"

"Okay," he conceded. "A little, maybe."

"We're basically stuck together, and quite frankly I'm tired of feeling so…edgy all the time. It would be nice if we could enjoy our time together." The instant the words left her mouth, she had a sudden and brilliant idea. It was absolutely ingenious!

"Uh-oh," he said, narrowing his eyes at her. "You look as though you've just had a lightbulb moment."

"I did. I don't know why I didn't think of it before."

"Why do I get the feeling I'm not going to like this?"

"On the contrary, I think you'll agree it's the only logical course of action."

"Okay," he said, looking skeptical. "Let's have it."

"I think, Alex, that I should sleep with you."

Eight

Alex's brows rose with surprise. "Say again?"

"Think about it," Sophie said. "After all this time, we're both wondering what it would be like."

"I am?"

She pinned him with a disbelieving look.

"Okay," he admitted. "I am."

"So maybe we should find out."

"And you think if we make love—"

"Sex, Alex, not love." Love had nothing, and would never have, anything to do with sex. "This is just...*chemistry*."

"My apologies. You think if we have *sex*, we won't be tense around each other anymore?"

"Exactly." In fact, the more she thought about it, the more logical the idea seemed.

"What if it doesn't?" he asked.

"Why wouldn't it? It's not as if our feelings toward each other are anything other than…"

"Chemistry?"

"Sexual *curiosity.*"

"So, if I had just had sex with you today in the woods, we wouldn't even be having this conversation?"

He folded his arms across his chest and studied her, brow furrowed. "I don't know about this."

"What do you mean, you don't know?" It was completely logical. What sane man would pass up an offer like that?

He shrugged. "It just sounds a little too easy."

"No, it doesn't. It's the perfect plan."

"You say that now, but I can't help thinking that something is bound to go wrong."

"What could possibly go wrong?"

"You could fall in love with me."

She bit her lip to hold in a laugh. "No offense, but I don't think we have to worry about that *ever* happening."

"Wow. I'm not sure if should feel relieved or insulted."

She shot him an exasperated look. Now he was just being obtuse. What man wouldn't jump at the chance for a night of no-strings-attached sex?

None she had ever known.

"What if once doesn't do the trick?" he asked.

"What if we have sex and we still feel this tension? Do we get to do it again?"

She couldn't really see that being a problem, not if they approached this logically. Not for her anyway. But for the sake of argument, she would humor him. "Let's just say that I'm open to the possibility."

"Fair enough."

"Well," she asked, anxious to settle this once and for all. "Are you in or out?"

He grinned. "What you're asking for would necessitate a bit of both, don't you think?"

She rolled her eyes. "Would you please be serious?"

He gave it a moment's thought, then said, "I'm trying to imagine a potential problem with this scenario, and honestly, I'm drawing a blank. No matter how I look at it, it's a win-win situation."

"So?"

He shrugged. "Yeah, sure, what the hell. I'm in."

"Splendid." It stunned her a little to realize what a huge weight this was off her shoulders. This was a *good* idea. A good plan. "Needless to say, we have to be discreet about this."

"Of course."

"*Especially* where Phillip is concerned."

"I agree." He rubbed his palms together and wiggled his brows at her. "So, Princess, when do we get started?"

She looked at her watch. "Tonight I have a charity function that I simply can't miss, and I won't be in until late this evening. Probably after midnight." To do this properly, she should at least be awake.

"Tomorrow, then?"

"Well, we'll be on the yacht with a full staff, so that won't work, then you have golf with Phillip and he mentioned taking you for dinner at the country club afterward. He's asked me to babysit Frederick until eleven."

He was beginning to look exasperated. "How about Thursday?"

"Thursday, you'll be at the hunting cabin and not back until Friday afternoon."

"And Friday is the black-tie charity deal, which I'm assuming will be another late one."

"At least midnight."

"How about Friday afternoon after we get back from the cabin?"

"Afternoons are difficult. Too many people around. Besides, I need a few hours to prepare for the evening."

"This is shaping up to be one stressful week, Your Highness."

He was right. This was a great idea, if they could just find the time to make it happen.

"You said you're watching Frederick until eleven tomorrow night?"

"That's right."

He grinned. "Eleven isn't too late. And I couldn't call myself a gentleman if I didn't offer to walk you home afterward."

That might work. "I suppose you couldn't."

"So, tomorrow at eleven?"

"Eleven it is." They could get this over and done with, then maybe they could actually enjoy each other's company for the remainder of his stay. And even better, they could walk away from this as friends.

In fact, the more she thought about it, the more convinced she was that this was exactly what they both needed.

She rose from the step, and he stood, too. "Now that we have that settled, I really need to get ready."

"You know, Princess, I think you're right. This is a good idea."

Of course it was. What man, especially one newly divorced and admittedly angry with all women, wouldn't see gratuitous sex as a good thing? And God knows that she hadn't been with a man in far too long. And contrary to what men seemed to think, women had needs, too. This would undoubtedly be a mutually beneficial arrangement.

Enough rationalizing, she told herself. She was doing the right thing.

"We'll leave for the yacht at nine," she told him. "So let's plan to meet in the foyer at our usual time."

"I'll be ready."

"The sun is quite intense this time of year, so make sure you bring sunscreen."

"Gotcha."

"Well then, I'll see you in the morning."

She turned toward the door, but he caught her forearm in his hand. "Hey, Princess."

She turned, and although she should have expected it, once again he caught her completely off guard. He cupped the back of her head, drew her to him and kissed her. But not a deep desperate joining like the last time. This was sweet and soft and maybe even a little tentative, his tongue barely sweeping the seam of her lips before he drew it back. Then he lingered for just another second or two before he finally pulled away.

"What was that for?" she asked, her words coming out soft and breathy. Her lips tingled and her legs were suddenly so wobbly that she almost had to sit back down.

He smiled and shrugged. "Consider it a sneak peek at what you have to look forward to tomorrow night."

He turned and started down the path toward the palace.

If that was what she had to look forward to, eleven o'clock tomorrow night couldn't come fast enough.

Sophie thought she had him. Thought she had gotten the best of him this time, but it was all part of the game.

He watched her until she reached her front door. She turned to flash him one last suggestive smile, then stepped inside and closed the door behind her.

He lingered for a moment, then turned and walked back to the palace. The dark clouds had blown over and the sun burned hot in the afternoon sky, but there was a cool breeze blowing in from the coast. A perfect afternoon for a walk. He needed the time to clear his head, get his priorities straight. Get himself back on track.

Sophie was good—he would give her that. For a second there, he had actually believed her seemingly heartfelt apology, had let himself think that she had changed. But that was the way women, especially women like her, operated. They said and did nothing without ulterior motives, every word and action carefully measured and executed to get exactly what they wanted.

That was why, when she'd first suggested they sleep together, he'd been convinced she was up to something. That she would lead him on briefly, then inevitably change her mind. But something in her eyes told him that wasn't the case. She wanted him. His seduction had been a success. And by making the first move, being the one to suggest they sleep together, she was operating under the delusion that she was the one in control, the one calling the shots.

And by the time she figured it out, it would be too late.

Eyes closed behind her darkest sunglasses, Sophie drifted in and out of consciousness, lulled by the gentle sway of the Irish Sea and the warm glow of the sun against her skin, hearing the occasional hum of a boat engine or the squawk of a gull. The spray of the wake against the hull.

Despite having been exhausted when she finally arrived home last night, sleep had evaded her. She had lain awake, her mind racing, the anticipation of her night with Alex teasing her like a gift under the tree at Christmastime. And he was one gift she couldn't wait to unwrap.

What would he feel like and how would he taste? Would it be as exciting as it had been ten years ago, or had youth been part of the magic back then? The element of danger?

Well, regardless of quality, she realized now that sleeping with Alex had been an inevitability. With her ingenious plan they would get it neatly out of the way and she would manage to retain complete control of the situation, which was really all she had wanted in the first place.

Speaking of Alex, she hadn't seen him in some time now. As soon as they'd boarded the boat, he had wandered off with the captain to get a look at the engine room. And because he seemed suitably amused, she had changed into her bathing suit, grabbed a deck chair and all but melted into it. Considering the current intensity of the sun, that had to have been at least two hours ago, but she was too relaxed to open her eyes, much less move a muscle to roll over and look through her bag for her watch.

The sun dipped behind a cloud and the gentle breeze cooled her sun-drenched skin. She waited patiently for the cloud to pass, but instead felt several drops of ice-cold liquid on her calves. Still mostly asleep, she crinkled her brow. Another series of drops landed on her left thigh, then a few more on her right.

The weather authority hadn't predicted rain for the rest of the week. And she found it awfully peculiar that this particular rain cloud had centered itself over her legs. Another icy splash hit her stomach and her eyes shot open. It wasn't a cloud blocking the sun—it was a person. A very tall person with wide shoulders.

With the sun behind him, his face was hidden in shadow, but there was only one man on board rude enough to wake her this way.

Alex stood over her chair, dipping his fingers in her iced tea and flicking it at her. "Wake up."

She groaned and closed her eyes. "Go away."

A few more icy drops hit her right arm.

"That is unbelievably juvenile," she mumbled.

"I'm bored."

She flung an arm across her face. "And how is that my problem?"

"You're my guide."

"I got you on the yacht—what more do you want?"

Freezing-cold tea landed with a sploosh on her stomach and she moved her arm to glare up at him. "*Stop* that!"

He was holding the glass over her, poised to dump the entire thing. She couldn't see his face, but she didn't doubt he was wearing the devilish grin that was becoming so familiar. In fact, he'd been wearing it this morning when they met in the foyer. He'd flashed her that smile, wiggled his brows at her and mouthed the words *you, me, eleven.*

As though she could forget.

"Is a little peace too much to ask for?" she asked.

"You've been out for almost three hours."

Three hours? Had it really been that long? She must have been more tired than she realized.

"Not that I haven't been enjoying the view," he said. There was a warm and sexy note to his voice and she had the distinct impression he wasn't talking about the landscape outside the yacht.

He shook the glass, rattling the ice. "You know I'll do it."

He probably would, and because it was obvious he wasn't going to go away, she had no choice but to humor him. "Fine. I'm awake."

He stepped out of the sun, and when she got a good look at him, her heart did a backflip with a triple twist.

When they'd met in the foyer he'd been wearing a polo shirt and canvas shorts. Now he was wearing a pair of Hawaiian-patterned swim trunks.

And nothing else.

Her blood instantly ran hot, pumping faster through her veins, and her eyes felt virtually glued to his body.

With his wet clothes sticking to him yesterday, she hadn't really gotten a good look at him. His chest was even more magnificent than she remembered. Strong and smooth, with just a dusting of hair on his pecks. And he had abs to die for. Well-defined and solid. She wondered absently how many hours a day he had to work to look this good, or if he just grew all these muscles naturally.

Come on, Soph, get a grip. So he wasn't wearing a shirt. Big deal. It was just a chest, for pity's sake. Nothing to lose her head over. It's not as if she'd never seen one before. Or this one in particular.

And she realized suddenly that she was openly staring. She swiftly peeled her gaze from his small, pink nipples and dragged her eyes upward, to his face, only to find that he was watching her watch him.

A quirky grin played at the corner of his mouth. "Something wrong?"

She blinked innocently. "Wrong?"

"You kind of zoned out there for a minute."

"I'm still half asleep," she snapped.

"You want to go for a swim? Wake up. *Cool off* a bit."

She glared at him. "Not particularly."

He shrugged, drawing her gaze to his strong, wide shoulders. They were looking a little pink. She peered over the top of her sunglasses and realized that they were more than a little pink. He was well on his way to a nasty-looking burn.

"Are you wearing sunblock?"

He shook his head. "Nope."

"How long have you had your shirt off?"

He shrugged. "A couple of hours, I guess. Why?"

If he was sunburned, he might not be able to… *perform* later. "I told you yesterday to wear sunblock. Let me guess—you didn't even bring any."

"I forgot."

She blew out an exasperated breath and sat up. She

had some in her bag, but it was only SPF 8, which would never suffice. "I'm sure there must be some belowdecks in the bedroom. Wait here. I'll go look."

She dragged herself up from the chair, adjusting her suit top. She could feel his eyes burning into her bare skin as she crossed the deck to the stairs. She wasn't wearing her skimpiest bikini; still, it didn't leave a heck of a lot to the imagination. She knew for a fact that he was getting quite an eyeful.

He could consider it—how did he phrase it?—as his own *sneak preview.* A glimpse of what he would be enjoying later tonight. And he would be enjoying it.

She didn't doubt that if Phillip were on board, he would cite anything more revealing than a modest one-piece inappropriate. But Phillip wasn't here. Besides, it felt good to be a little rebellious for a change.

She padded down the stairs and across the plush bedroom carpet to the private head. She found what she was looking for in the cabinet below the sink. SPF 30 lotion. Just to be safe.

She turned to leave, startled to find the bedroom door now closed, and Alex standing in front of it.

"Nice bedroom," he said, but he wasn't looking around the room. His eyes were glued to her body.

"What are you doing in here?" she said in a loud whisper. Was he trying to get them caught?

He started walking slowly toward her. "Helping you look for the sunblock."

"I already found it." She noticed that not only had

he closed the door, but he'd locked it, too. "Is this your idea of being discreet?"

"What do you expect? That bathing suit is… *wow.*" He looked her up and down as he moved closer, devouring her with his eyes. "Look me in the eye and tell me you didn't wear it just to tease me."

That was exactly what she'd done. She just hadn't anticipated it being quite so effective. "We can't be in here together."

"Yet here we are," he said, moving closer still, and other than vaulting over the bed to get to the door, she had no way to escape. And she had never been terribly athletic.

"We said eleven tonight," she reminded him.

"Eleven tonight is the main course." A grin quirked up one corner of his mouth. "Consider this an appetizer."

And what a delicious treat he would be, but she really couldn't allow him to do this. Not here, where, for all she knew, Phillip had the employees spying on her. A skimpy bikini was one thing, but a tryst belowdecks with a client was pushing it. "I appreciate the thought, but it's really going to have to wait."

His eyes raked over her, dilated and intense, like an animal anticipating the kill. Then he reached out for her and the instant his fingers brushed her hip, when her skin tingled with awareness and her knees went weak, she knew it was pointless to try and fight it. She didn't *want* to fight it anymore. It felt too bloody good.

"Still want me to leave?"

"You have five minutes."

He reached for the opposite hip, cupping it in his palm, his skin so hot to the touch she nearly gasped. "This is going to take a lot longer than five minutes."

He pulled her to him, her breasts brushing against the solid, unyielding wall of his chest. Her nipples tingled and stiffened into two painfully erect, yearning buds.

He dipped his head and nuzzled the side of her throat, just below her ear, then he nipped her lobe lightly and the bottle she'd been holding slipped from her fingers and landed with a muffled thump on the carpet.

"You know," he said, his breath hot on her neck, his lips brushing her skin as he spoke, "you're even more beautiful than you were ten years ago."

"Coincidentally," she told him, her voice coming out breathy and soft, "so are you."

His hands slipped lower, sliding around to cup her behind. A purr of pleasure worked its way up from deep inside of her. She leaned into him, resting her face against his smooth cheek, savoring the sensations of skin against skin. It had been so long since someone—anyone—had touched her like this, so tenderly. Every second that passed felt like an eternity. She waited for his next move, for him to slip his hands inside her bikini bottoms. The thought of him touching her that way made her dizzy and lightheaded, as though she would pass out from the anticipation of his next move.

Was this her idea of maintaining control of the situation? It was obvious that, right now anyway, Alex was calling the shots. And even worse, she didn't care.

She actually liked it, even though the concept went against everything she ever believed or was taught.

With barely more than gentle tug she was pressed against the length of Alex's body. His skin felt smooth and hot, and she could feel his heart thumping the wall of his chest.

"Still want me to stop?" he asked.

"I want you to kiss me."

A slow smile curled his lips. "I can do that."

He lowered his head nuzzled her cheek. His skin smelled warm and salty from the sea air and faintly of coconut.

Wait a minute. *Coconut?*

She leaned in and sniffed his shoulder. He *did.* He smelled like sunblock!

She looked up at him.

His brow furrowed. "What?"

She sniffed him again and asked, "Are you wearing sunblock?"

The smile went from sexy to devious in the blink of an eye. *"Maybe."*

"You are, aren't you? Why did you tell me you weren't?"

"What sane man would pass up the chance to have you rub sunblock all over him? Although I never imagined it would get us alone in the bedroom together. That was just dumb luck."

She gave him a playful shove. "You're a creep."

He just smiled. He was a creep, but an adorable one.

"We need to get back up on deck before someone—"

There was a loud rap on the bedroom door and she nearly jumped out of her skin.

A voice called, "Lunch is served, Your Highness."

So much for not being caught in a compromising position. They had to have figured out by now that Alex was in there with her.

She called back, "I'll be up in a minute."

Alex exhaled an exasperated breath. "So much for an appetizer."

"I told you this wasn't the time." She pushed lightly against his chest and he let go of her.

"Maybe, but you weren't putting up much of a fight."

In all fairness, she hadn't been. In fact, her actions could have easily been interpreted as encouragement. "We should leave the room one at a time."

He folded his arms across his chest. "That won't look suspicious."

She straightened her bikini bottoms and checked her reflection in the mirror on the bedroom door. Her cheeks were flushed, but that could easily be explained away by her three-hour nap in the sun. "You have a better idea?"

It was obvious, by his lack of response, that he didn't.

"Besides, it looks as though you could use a minute or two to—" she nodded at the recent and conspicuously tight fit of his swim trunks "*—cool off.*"

"I was thinking more along the lines of a cold shower."

"Well, that's what you get for bending the rules," she said, crossing the room to the door.

"What rules are those?" he asked.

"The rules of nutrition."

A grin quirked up the corners of his lips. *"Nutrition."*

She opened the door and grinned back at him. "No snacking between meals."

Nine

Alex had no time to be alone with Sophie after lunch, although not for lack of trying, but the staff always seemed to be around. Just before three they docked in the marina and were driven back to the palace. He barely had time to change before he and Phillip were off to the golf course.

Under normal circumstances Alex enjoyed golf, but today he was distracted. And even though they hadn't played together in years, Phillip noticed.

"Off your game today?" he said, when they got back to the clubhouse. "I remember you being slightly better at this."

"Normally I am. I'm a bit sunburned from sailing." It wasn't a total lie. His shoulders were a bit tender, despite the sunblock he'd put on not long after they'd left the marina—which Sophie would have known if she hadn't passed out in a deck chair the minute they boarded. And honestly, he doubted she was as scandalized as she wanted him to believe. She'd wanted him in that bedroom just as much as he wanted to be there.

And as much as he was enjoying all the teasing and foreplay, he was ready for the main event tonight. It seemed to be all he could think about, which was the real reason he'd shot such a pathetic nine holes today. But he couldn't exactly tell Phillip that.

"Would you like the palace physician to take a look at it?" Phillip asked.

"No, thanks. I'm sure I'll be fine by tomorrow."

They dropped off their gear and headed to the lounge to wait for Hannah. An attractive young waitress took their drink order, but Phillip barely seemed to notice her. He was polite, but distant. The complete opposite of the Phillip from college. Back then if he found a woman attractive, he wasn't shy about letting her know. Now it would seem that he had eyes only for his wife.

Alex wondered what it would be like to love someone so much that he didn't even look at other women. What Phillip and Hannah had must have been very special.

"You had a good time on the yacht today?" Phillip asked.

"I did." An exceptionally good time.

"I seem to recall you mentioned having a yacht, too."

"I used to. My ex got that in the divorce." She would have tried to get the family jewels if they weren't attached. And he wasn't talking about his grandmother's diamonds. "It was good to get back out on the water."

"How are you and Sophie getting on?"

"Good. Sophie is…" He struggled for the words to describe her. But all he could come up with was sexy and smart and stubborn as hell, but somehow he didn't think that was what Phillip would want to hear. So instead he said, "An excellent hostess."

If Phillip noticed the pause, he let it slide. "Sophie knows more of this island, of the country, than anyone."

"I have learned a lot the last few days."

"I'll bet you have," Phillip said, and Alex had the distinct impression he knew more than he was letting on. But Hannah walked in just then and they stood to greet her. From there they moved on to the royal family's private dining room. The waitress had just left with their food order when Phillip's cell phone rang.

He reached to answer and Hannah shot him a stern look.

He checked the display and said, "I know we have a no-phone rule at dinner, but I really need to take this."

"Fine." She waved him away with a grudging smile. "Go answer it."

He rose from his chair. "If you'll excuse me for a moment."

Hannah sighed and watched him walk away, phone to his ear. "That's what I get for marrying a king, I suppose." She turned to Alex, laying a hand on his forearm. "At least this will give us a moment to chat. Are you enjoying your stay with us?"

"Very much. It's exactly what I needed."

She gave his arm a sympathetic pat. "Phillip said it's been rough for you."

She was so sweet, so kind. There was something refreshingly...*simple* about her. Elegant and refined, yet amazingly down-to-earth. A stranger on the street would never guess she was royalty, and several years Phillip's junior, they might have a tough time buying that she was a wife and mother. Of course, there probably wasn't anyone in the country, in much of the world even, who wouldn't recognize Queen Hannah. She was regarded around the globe as a compassionate royal and tireless philanthropist.

"No divorce is ever fun," he said with a shrug. "I am glad it's over though."

"If you need anything at all you be sure to let us know." She gave his arm a quick squeeze, then drew her hand back. "Have you and Sophie had time to get reacquainted?"

He could swear there was a suggestive lilt to her tone. "Yes. She's very much like I remember her."

She sipped her water, peering at him over the rim of her glass, and asked, "Does she know how you feel about her?"

And here he thought he'd done a pretty good job of

hiding his feelings. Either he was far more transparent than he thought or Her Highness was quite perceptive. "What makes you think I have feelings for her?"

She shrugged. "Something about that first night at dinner. A subtle vibe I was getting."

The only vibe he'd been giving off then had been derision. Maybe she was mistaking contempt for attraction.

Maybe he was, too.

"Sophie may be tough on the outside," Hannah said, "but don't let her fool you. She has a soft center. But I have the feeling you already know that. In fact, I think you've known that for a very long time."

She obviously suspected they had some sort of history, but did she know just how personal?

"Me and Sophie," Alex said. "It's…complicated."

"Relationships usually are, Alex. Even more so when you're dealing with royalty."

Wasn't that the truth.

He wondered if Phillip had the same suspicions. If he and Hannah had discussed it. And if so, why hadn't he ever said anything to Alex?

Hannah seemed to read his mind. "Phillip doesn't know. At least, he's never said anything to me about it."

And considering the nature of Alex and Sophie's relationship, hopefully Phillip wouldn't figure it out. Even though this sexual liaison had been her idea, he doubted that argument would hold much water with Phillip.

"So, being newly divorced and all, I suppose your

relationship with Sophie will most likely be... *fleeting*," Hannah said.

"I would imagine so." That was a polite and diplomatic way to say they were having an affair. And he wouldn't lie to her by denying it. It's not as if it had been his idea.

All right, maybe it had been. But his plan had been to seduce her against her will, not ask her permission. But either way, he was getting what he wanted. She may have thought she wouldn't fall in love with him, but she had no idea who she was dealing with.

Although he had to admit that this was feeling less and less like a plot for revenge and more like... Well, honestly, he wasn't sure *what* it felt like.

"That's a shame," Hannah said. "I get the feeling you two would be very good for each other."

There had been a time when he would have agreed with her. But this time he wouldn't be sticking around long enough to find out.

"I would imagine you'd prefer I didn't say anything to Phillip about this."

"I would never ask you to keep secrets from your husband," he said.

"But you would really appreciate it if I didn't. I don't tell Phillip every little thing. Besides, Sophie is one of my dearest friends, and if you hurt her, Phillip's wrath would pale in comparison to what I would do to you."

"I'll consider myself warned," he said.

She smiled. "Good."

Phillip reappeared at that moment and reclaimed his chair. "Good news! The meeting I had planned for first thing tomorrow has been cancelled."

Alex wasn't sure why that was such good news, and his confusion must have shown, because Phillip added, "No meeting in the morning means we can get an early start on our trip."

"Oh, great," he said, even though leaving earlier meant less time tonight with Sophie.

"In fact, I see no reason why we should wait until tomorrow," Phillip said. "The cabin is only an hour away. We should leave tonight."

Normally Sophie loved babysitting her nephew, but tonight she'd been edgy. She'd put him to bed at eight, and hadn't stopped pacing past the window, watching for Phillip and Hannah's car. By nine-thirty, when it pulled up the driveway, an hour and a half early, *thank God,* she'd practically worn a path in the carpet. She forced herself to take a seat on the sofa and crack open the book she'd brought with her. It seemed to take them forever to get up the stairs to their suite.

"How is my little angel?" Hannah asked the instant they were through the door.

"Sleeping," Sophie said, rising from her seat, expecting Alex to follow them inside. She waited, thinking maybe he was just a few steps behind, but Phillip closed the door behind him.

How was Alex going to offer to walk her home if he wasn't there?

"How was he?" Phillip asked.

"He?"

"Frederick."

"Oh, right. He was good. Perfect, as usual."

"I'm so glad," Hannah said. "He's cutting his bottom teeth, so I was afraid he might be cranky."

"How was dinner?" Sophie asked, when what she really wanted to know was where the heck was Alex?

"Pleasant," Phillip said, then he tagged her with a kiss on the cheek on his way to the bedroom. "I'm going to go pack."

Pack? "Are you going somewhere?"

Hannah dropped her purse on the coffee table and collapsed onto the sofa. "Phillip and Alex have decided to leave for the cabin tonight instead of waiting until morning."

They were leaving *tonight?*

No, no, no! They couldn't leave tonight. She and Alex had plans. They were going to have sex, dammit. "It's kind of late, isn't it?"

Hannah shrugged. "You know men and their insatiable desire to bear arms."

She bit the inside of her cheek so hard she drew blood. "You don't care that he's going to leave you and Frederick alone all night?"

"It's not a big deal. I'll probably just go straight to bed anyway. I'm exhausted."

There had to be a way to stop this. She had to talk

to Alex. "Well, if you don't need me for anything else, I'll be heading home."

"Sure, Sophie," Hannah said, her voice already heavy with sleep and her lids drooping. "Thanks so much for watching the munchkin."

"Tell my brother I said to have a good time."

She let herself out of their suite, then left the family residence, but rather than take the stairs down, she crossed to the guest wing and rapped on Alex's door.

He opened it, looking apologetic, and said, "I know you're probably upset."

She stepped inside and shut the door behind her. "You're going *tonight?*"

"This is so not my fault."

"Alex!"

"What was I supposed to do? He said he wanted to go early. What reason could I give him to wait until the morning?"

"You could have come up with *something.*"

He looked at his watch. "I have to pack. I'm meeting him downstairs in fifteen minutes."

He walked to the bedroom and she followed him.

Fifteen minutes wasn't very long, but they could probably pull it off. But if they were only going to do this once, she didn't want to rush.

"By the way, Hannah knows," Alex said.

"Knows what?"

He stepped into the closet and pulled down a small travel case from the shelf. "About us."

"What?" Sophie stopped in her tracks. "What did you say to her?"

"Nothing." He tossed the case on the bed and began shoving clothes in it. "She approached me about it, said she picked up on a vibe that first night at dinner."

Oh, not good. "Did she say it in front of Phillip?"

He shook his head. "He was away from the table taking a call. She told me she wouldn't say anything to him. And she more or less threatened to do me bodily harm if I hurt you."

"*Hannah* did?"

"Yeah, it was weird. She seems so sweet and unassuming." He stepped into the bathroom and she followed him.

"Does she know the extent of it?"

"If she does, she came to that conclusion on her own. We didn't talk specifics." He gathered his toiletries and dropped them into a case. "Although we did determine that it's temporary."

"And she's not going to tell Phillip?"

"That's what she said."

That was good at least.

He zipped his case and brushed past her to the bedroom, and goodness did he smell good. Like fresh air and sunshine.

She followed him, watching as he stuffed the case into his bag and zipped it closed. It wasn't fair. This was supposed to be *their* night. This wouldn't be so bad if she had at least gotten to enjoy that appetizer this afternoon. Or who knows, maybe that would have been worse.

He checked his watch and grabbed the bag from the bed. "I have to go."

She didn't want him to go, but what could she do? Beg him not to leave? Implore him to fabricate some excuse to leave the following morning instead? She wouldn't give him the satisfaction of knowing just how important this had become to her. After all, she didn't want to give him false hope. Because if anyone was going to be doing any falling in love, it would most likely be him.

It had happened before.

"Well, have a good time shooting things," she said.

"I'll try to talk Phillip into coming home Thursday," he said.

"If you do, and I'm free, perhaps we can spend the evening together."

He grinned. "If you're free, huh?" Then he hooked his free arm around her waist, tugged her against him and planted a kiss on her that curled her toes and melted her bones. When he abruptly let go, she nearly sank to the floor. "Think about that while I'm gone, and tell me you won't be free."

She opened her mouth to reply, but by the time her brain cleared and she formulated a snappy comeback, he was already gone.

Ten

Alex had a good time at the hunting cabin. It was his and Phillip's first chance to really catch up and speak frankly about what they had been up to since college. And it made him realize how much he missed their friendship since they had drifted apart. Jonah would always be Alex's best friend, his brother, but it was a nice change to hang out with someone who didn't know him so well. Someone not so quick to judge Alex, but instead observe his life with an unbiased opinion.

But late Thursday evening Hannah called to say that Frederick had a fever, and even though the doctor said it was nothing to worry about, Phillip insisted on coming home.

"I hope you don't mind," Phillip said as they loaded their bags into the car.

"Of course not," Alex told him. "Family comes first."

"The physician said it could be a reaction to his teething, and there's nothing to be done, but I feel better if I'm there with them."

If Alex had kids, he was sure he would feel the same way. And had he and his ex produced children together, they would have been pawns in the divorce. One more weapon for her to use against him. And he didn't doubt that she would have. She'd had no problem lying to his family and twisting the truth. And even worse, they seemed to trust her over their own flesh and blood.

His ex spent years spinning her web of lies, and by the time he realized what she'd been up to, it was too late. She had everyone snowed.

And yes, he admitted to himself as he and Phillip climbed in the car, he had unfairly transferred some of that pent up animosity on to Sophie. If his only motivation for sleeping with her had been revenge, would he have missed her company this past day? And would her face be the first thing he wanted to see when they got back to the palace? Which seemed to take an immeasurably long time for some reason. The hour drive felt more like two, but his watch confirmed that it was indeed only ten forty-five.

He wondered if Sophie was *available.* Or if she might have already gone to bed.

When they walked inside, Hannah was in the foyer pacing, a sleeping Frederick sprawled limply in her arms.

"I just got him to sleep," she whispered as Phillip leaned in to kiss her. He pressed a cheek to his son's forehead. Checking for a temperature, Alex supposed. He recalled seeing his sister do that with his niece and nephew. It was a reminder of what a devoted family man Phillip had become. And for the first time, Alex wondered if he had missed out on something special by refusing to have children.

Not that he couldn't still have them with someone else.

"He still feels warm," Phillip whispered back, caressing his son's flushed cheek.

"Every time I try to lay him down he has a fit. My arms ache from carrying him all day."

"Give him to me and I'll try to lay him down."

She transferred Frederick into his arms.

It still struck Alex to see Phillip so settled. And content to be that way. "See you tomorrow," he told Alex, then carried the baby up the stairs.

"I'm sorry to make you come home early," Hannah told him. "I would have been fine alone for another night, but Phillip is very devoted to his son. More than most fathers I think, because his own parents were so absent from his life. He and Sophie were raised by nannies and housekeepers. I think it left deep scars in them both."

"Speaking of Sophie," he said, glancing at his watch, "do you think it's too late to call her?"

He didn't say why, and he hoped Hannah wouldn't ask.

"She's not home. She helped me with Fredrick for while, but when she heard Phillip was on his way home, she left. She said something about having a date."

A date? She knew for a fact that he was coming back to the palace, but rather than wait, she'd found someone else to occupy her time? Not that he cared either way.

And if he didn't care, why did he feel as though he'd just been kicked in the gut?

"I hope it was all right to tell you that. I mean…I don't want to cause any hurt feelings. But since what you and she have is casual, I just figured…" She shrugged.

"It's fine," Alex told her, because it should have been. He had no expectation of fidelity from a woman he wasn't technically seeing. "I just had a question about the fund-raiser tomorrow night."

"Do you have her cell number?" Hannah asked. "I'm sure you can reach her."

"It's not important. I can talk to her tomorrow."

"Well, I should get upstairs and help Phillip."

"I'll walk you up," he said.

They walked up together, then parted ways at the top of the stairs. She disappeared into the residence, and he walked to the guest wing. Once inside his room he fixed himself a drink and walked over to the window, looking out across the dark yard to Sophie's residence. The exterior was brightly lit, and several of the upstairs lights were burning. It looked as though she was home. It was possible she wasn't really on a date. She may have only told Hannah that to take the focus off her and Alex.

And if that was true, he should at least let her know that he was back.

He walked to the phone and dialed the number she'd left him on the itinerary. Wilson answered, and when Alex asked for Sophie, he was curtly informed him that the princess was out for the evening.

Alex thanked him and hung up, feeling like an ass for calling in the first place. And even more of an ass for caring where Sophie was or who she might be with. And the last thing he felt like doing was sitting around sulking about it.

He carried his drink to the bedroom and switched on the light beside the bed, and felt, for the second time that day, as if he'd been poleaxed. Lying on top of the covers, curled in a ball and sleeping soundly, was Sophie.

He had no idea what she was doing there when she was supposed to be out on a date, but he couldn't deny he was happy to see her. So happy that it was more than a little disconcerting. It wasn't supposed to feel this good. Just seeing her, knowing she was there.

By being here, she was in her own way telling him just how much she wanted to be with him. And he didn't think he would ever look at her quite the same way again. Or for that matter, himself.

He set down his drink and sat on the edge of the bed to take off his shoes and socks, then lay down and rolled on his side, facing her. She didn't budge. And although he wanted to wake her, he liked her this way. Quiet and vulnerable. And peaceful. For a few minutes he lay there just looking at her, memorizing her face, wondering what the hell he was doing. What he was getting himself into.

Just to see what she would do, he leaned closer and brushed his lips against her cheek, the tip of her nose. She wrinkled her nose and mumbled something in her sleep.

He brushed his lips against hers, whispered, "Wake up, Sleeping Beauty."

Her eyes fluttered open, hazy and unfocused at first, but when she saw him lying there, she smiled. "You're back."

"Boring date?"

She looked confused, then she laughed softly. "Oh, yeah. I just told Hannah that to throw her off. Then I sneaked in here to wait for you." She yawned and stretched out beside him. "I guess I was tired."

She was dressed in a pair of white cropped pants and a pink silk tank that rode up to expose a sliver of soft, deeply tanned stomach, and her hair was pulled back in a ponytail. She looked young and sassy. And completely irresistible. He reached up to brush a wisp of dark hair back from her face. Any excuse to touch her.

"So, here we are," she said.

"Here we are." And she had come to him.

She touched his face, stroking his cheek with her fingers. "I'm sorry that Frederick isn't feeling well. But the kid has great timing."

He wrapped an arm around her and tugged her against him. "How are we on time, by the way?"

She folded her arms around his neck, shifted closer, winding her legs around his. Her body felt long and soft, and warm from sleep. "You mean, when do I have to leave?"

"Exactly."

"Phillip and Hannah have no idea that I'm here, and I told Wilson that I would be staying at the palace tonight."

That was just the answer he was hoping for, because it was going to take the entire night to do all the things to her that he'd been imagining.

She burrowed closer, nuzzling her face against his neck. "Do you remember the first night I came to your room? The last time you stayed here? The way we just kissed and touched and talked all night and didn't make love until the sun was coming up?"

He slipped his hand under her top, stroking her back. "I remember."

She tunneled her fingers through his hair and nibbled on his throat, her breath hot on his skin. "I'd like to do that again."

"Except we're not making love," he reminded her. "We're having sex."

"There is that," she said, and smiled up at him, a look of pure mischief in her eyes. "And I could probably do without all the talking."

He brushed his lips against hers. "So that leaves kissing and touching."

"And sex. Although I'm not sure I want to wait all night for that." She arched against him, nipping his lower lip with her teeth.

He cupped her breast, trapping her nipple between his thumb and forefinger. It was high and firm and fit perfectly in his palm. "How's that?"

She gazed up at him, lids heavy with desire. "On second thought, why don't we just forget about that first night and make some new memories instead." Then she grabbed his head, pulled his face to hers and kissed him. Slow and deep and long. And she was already working on the buttons of his shirt, undressing him.

If they were only doing this once and they had all night, he'd be damned if he was going to let her rush him. He grabbed her wrists, tried to put her arms back up around his neck, but she wiggled free. "Slow down."

She was back at his buttons. "I don't want to slow down. I want you naked."

He made a move to grab her arm and she nipped at his hand. He yanked away, and didn't doubt for a second that she would have actually bitten him. Just for that, she wouldn't be seeing him naked for a very long time.

When she had his shirt unbuttoned and reached for his fly, he grabbed both of her wrists. He pinned her arms over her head and rolled on top of her, stilling her with his weight.

"That isn't fair," she said, struggling to free herself. But she wasn't struggling so hard that he thought she really wanted to get away. He could see that if he didn't let her know who was calling the shots, this night was going to be long, unending power struggle.

He grinned down at her. "No one ever said anything about playing fair."

He kissed her again, just as slow and deep as she'd kissed him, and it wasn't long before she stopped struggling, before she melted into the mattress beneath him. He let go of her arms and she wrapped them around his neck, digging her fingers through his hair, feeding off his mouth. She was even more fiery and passionate than he remembered.

He pulled her shirt up and over her head, and tossed it onto the floor. She was wearing a pink push-up bra constructed entirely of lace that left nothing to the imagination. Her nipples were small and dark and tightly puckered. He'd never seen anything so beautiful.

He lowered his head and nipped at one with his teeth. Sophie gasped and arched up against him. And when he tried to lift his head, she forced it back down again. And this time he decided he would humor her. He yanked one side of her bra down, baring her breast, and took her into his mouth. She moaned and arched up closer to his mouth, and because he liked the reaction he got, he did the same to the opposite side. He licked and nipped at her skin, until Sophie was writhing underneath him.

She tried to guide his mouth to hers, struggling for control again, so instead he slipped down her body, nuzzling his face against her rib cage and her stomach. He got up on his knees to unfasten her pants. She reached for him, trying to get to his zipper again, and he shot her a stern look. "Don't make me tie you down."

A sexy smile curled her mouth and her eyes were an inferno. "You say that like it's a bad thing."

Maybe later, but right now he had other things planned.

Instead she reached back to unsnap her bra and tossed it somewhere in the vicinity of her shirt. Her breasts were perfect. Small and firm but soft.

He leaned forward, gave each one another kiss, then worked his way lower, across her stomach as he eased her pants down her legs, until all that was left was one tiny scrap of pink lace that could barely pass for a pair of panties. And underneath it was nothing but bare, smooth, golden tan skin.

He nuzzled her stomach, just above the top edge of the lace. She let her head fall back against the pillow. She had the most amazing throat, long and slender and graceful. He kissed her through the lace, blowing hot air against her skin and she made a soft mewling sound deep in her throat. Her scent was light and fresh and feminine.

He hooked his thumbs under the edge of the waistband, sliding the lace down her legs and off her feet, and tossed it over his shoulder. Then he sat back on his heels and just looked at her.

She gazed up at him, her eyes glassy and confused. "What?"

"Nothing."

"Why are you staring at me like that?"

"I just want to look at you."

"Oh. Okay."

He sat there for a minute, taking in every inch of her perfect body. Her feet were small for a woman of her height and surprisingly petite, her ankles slender and delicate-looking. And damn, her legs were long. He couldn't wait to feel them locked around him.

He leaned forward, kissed the inside of one knee.

"Why am I the only one naked?" she asked.

"Because it's not my turn yet."

"Says who?"

"Me."

"Oh, I get it. You're shy and you're afraid to admit it."

He pressed his lips to the opposite knee. "If that didn't work on you, Princess, do you really think it would work on me?"

She looked only slightly defeated, like she'd known it was a long shot but had to try anyway. "I don't suppose you could drop the 'Princess' and 'Your Highness' thing, and just call me Sophie."

"I'll think about it..." He ran his tongue up her

inner thigh, making her shudder, then looked down at her and grinned. "…Your Highness."

She might have balked, were she not so turned on, but her body didn't lie. He could see how slick and ready she was for him. And God knows he was ready, too. It had been too damned long. Too long since he felt so connected to a woman. Since sex had been this…fun.

And he didn't want to rush things, but Sophie seemed to think he was taking things a bit too slow.

"Touch me, Alex," she said in a pleading voice, so he brushed her lightly with his fingers, where she was slippery and warm. She whimpered softly, biting her lip. He went one step further, sliding one finger inside her.

She sucked in a breath and her hips rocked up toward his hand, forcing him in deeper.

"You want more?"

"Yes," she hissed, her eyes bleary and unfocused, and he loved that he was making her feel good, that it was so damned easy.

He gave her one more, then a third, but he could see it still wasn't enough. He lowered his head and touched her with his tongue and was rewarded with a low, throaty moan. Then he took her in his mouth and she nearly vaulted off the bed. She tasted sweeter and more delicious than his favorite dessert, and was a hell of a lot more satisfying. Then he felt those amazing legs hooking over his shoulders, locking him in, as if he'd actually stop. It didn't get any better than this.

He kept his touch light, just a flick of his tongue or tug with his mouth, to make it last, because he didn't want it to be over too fast and it was obvious she was almost there already. Her fingers were tangled in his hair, her head thrown back and her eyes closed, her heels digging into his back.

Careful as he was though, he could feel her slipping, coming closer, then she tensed and arched up, crushing his head between her thighs. Her body coiled and locked, and a deep shudder rocked through her. But damn, he didn't want it to be over so soon. He wanted to see just how far he could take her. So instead of stopping, he increased the pressure of his mouth, of his tongue. She made a sound of protest and tried to push his head away, press her legs together, but he held her down. And after a minute of that, she was no longer pushing him away, and instead pulling him closer. Making soft, desperate, pleading sounds. And she shattered almost instantly.

He kissed his way up her stomach. Her skin was warm and flushed and he could feel her heart thumping, the blood rushing through her veins.

She sighed, sprawling limply across the comforter. "That felt *so* good."

He kissed and nipped his way upward, through the valley between her perfect breasts. To her throat and chin, and when he got to her face, he grinned down at her. "Lucky for you, Your Highness, I'm just getting warmed up."

Eleven

So much for his using her name. But she felt so damned good that right now, she didn't care what he called her. She was too limp to move, to even open her eyes. "That's never happened to me before."

"Which part?" Alex asked.

"The multiple part."

"Really?" There was a note of both disbelief and pride in his voice.

"As a rule, I try to limit my orgasms one at a time."

"Why is that?"

"It's never good to set the bar too high. You only end up disappointed." In fact, he had probably just ruined her for other men.

She was so relaxed and sated, she could lay there

like that for hours, but she realized, she was being terribly selfish. She had been *thoroughly* satisfied, and he hadn't even taken off his clothes yet.

She looped her arms around his neck and pulled him down for a kiss, and told him, "It's your turn to get undressed."

He grinned down at her. "Says who?"

"Me." Then she added firmly, "*Now.*"

Without argument he sat up and she sat up beside him, legs curled under her, to watch. He shrugged out of his shirt and dropped it beside the bed. He fished his wallet from his pants pocket and set it on the night table, then unfastened them and kicked them off. His boxers were the last to go, and when he slid them off, she sighed with satisfaction. She thought she'd recalled everything about him, but her memory didn't do him justice.

"Lie down," she said, pushing him onto his back. "It's my turn to look at you."

He'd been so determined to overpower her, she was a little surprised when he let her straddle his thighs, pinning him to the mattress. And for a moment she just let her eyes wander over him, taking it all in, burning it in her memory. So this time, after he was gone, she wouldn't forget. She would always remember that, no matter how short a period of time, just how good this had been.

His body was just so…perfect. So beautiful. More so because of the man on the inside. And just for tonight, he was all hers. Inside and out.

She was almost sorry it couldn't be longer, even though she knew it was better this way.

When simply looking at him wasn't enough, she put her hands on him, following the path her eyes had just taken. She touched his arms and his chest and his stomach. And when she'd made her way down to his erection, she paused for a moment, just looking, then she took him in her hand, squeezing gently. He sighed and shifted under her, his eyes slipped closed. His skin felt hot and smooth and alive with sensation.

"You're beautiful," she said. "Is it okay to call a man beautiful? I mean, I don't want to give you a complex."

"Keep touching me like that and you can call it anything you want."

She closed her hand around him and stroked, up the entire length of him, then back down again. "Like this?"

He answered her with a soft groan, gazing up at her through eyes half closed with arousal. There was nothing she loved more than experimenting with the male body, learning every trick and fetish. Exactly what to do to make him feel good. And for a while that's what she did. Touched and teased him, using her hands and mouth. But after a bit of that he caught her face between his hands and kissed her, then whispered in her ear, "As good as this feels, I really want to be inside you."

"You have protection, I hope." It would be a bloody shame if they came this far, only to have to stop.

"In my wallet," he said, nodding toward the table.

She did love a man who came prepared. She

grabbed his wallet and opened it. There was a thick wad of cash inside, and half a dozen credit cards. And a condom. Several in fact.

She recognized the packaging as American, meaning he'd brought them with him. Which didn't necessarily mean he'd been planning this. What single man in this day and age didn't carry prophylactics?

She plucked one out, then grabbed a second, just in case, and tossed his wallet back onto the table. She tore one of the wrappers open with her teeth and asked, "May I do the honors?"

He grinned up at her, a devilishly hungry smile. "Knock yourself out, Princess."

She rolled it on, *very* slowly, knowing by the look on his face that she was driving him crazy. Which was exactly the point of course. And when she was finished, he said, "Make love to me."

She didn't want him to know how real this was for her. How it felt like so much more than just sex. Just as it had ten years ago, when she still felt as though she had her entire life ahead of her.

He wrapped both hands around her hips, guiding her, and she lowered herself over him, slowly taking him inside her, savoring the sensation of being filled. She was still hot and slick and her muscles hugged him firmly as she rose up, then sank back down again.

Alex ran his hands up her sides to her breasts, cupping them in his palms, pinching her nipples lightly, making her shiver. He pulled her down so he could reach them with his mouth, flicking his tongue against the pebble hard peak of one nipple, then the other. Then he pulled her mouth to his and kissed her, one of those deep, soul-searching kisses that curled her toes and make her head spin. Then she realized, it wasn't just her head spinning. Alex was rolling her over without missing a beat or interrupting their rhythm, and the next thing she knew, she was on her back, pinned by his weight, and he was grinning down at her.

To hell with making love. She wanted this. She wanted it rough and desperate. And she could feel herself letting go, losing what little control she had left, arching against him, legs twined around his hips. Digging her nails into his back. Moaning and writhing. And she couldn't do a thing to stop it. She was a puppet and Alex pulled the strings.

She lost track of time after that, lost track of herself. Everything she smelled and felt and heard, every taste and touch, all melted together and became a blur. It built and climbed, higher and higher. And when she thought she couldn't stand it anymore, when it was unbearable, she went higher still.

Then Alex said her name. "Sophie, look at me."

The instant their eyes locked, she blew apart, taking him along with her. Her release welled up from a place deep inside her, grabbed hold and didn't let go.

Her body was still quaking with tiny aftershocks when Alex rolled over beside her. They were both breathing heavy, hearts thumping wildly.

"I don't know about you," Alex said, "but I'm not tense anymore."

Nope, she was as limp as a wet noodle. "I guess it worked."

"I guess."

And if they were to do this only once, they had certainly gone down in a blaze of glory. Only now, doing it just once wasn't sounding like such a hot idea anymore. The idea of touching him, making love to him again, had her heart beating faster.

Maybe instead of one time, they should limit it to one *night.* Since neither had anything better to do anyway.

She rolled on her side and curled up to him, draping one leg over both of his, playing with the soft hair on his chest. "Alex?"

"Hmm?"

"I have a problem."

He looked down at her, brow furrowed. "What kind of problem?"

"I'm feeling tense again."

The hint of a grin tipped up one corner of his mouth. "Well, then, Princess. We'll just have to do something about that.

. . .

At 5:00 a.m., before any of the family were up, and running on barely an hour of sleep, Sophie slipped out of Alex's bed, threw on her clothes and tiptoed down the stairs. She was only a dozen steps from the door and almost home free when Hannah walked out of the kitchen, Frederick awake and gurgling happily on her shoulder, and caught her red-handed sneaking out.

"My, you're up early," Hannah said, flashing Sophie a wry smile.

"You, too. The munchkin seems to be feeling better."

"His fever is gone and it looks as though his teeth are beginning to break through." She patted his back. "You know, you're lucky."

"Lucky?"

"Phillip usually does the morning feeding."

"Oh?"

"If you don't want him to know about you and Alex, you probably shouldn't spend the night."

Probably not. "Well, I should get home, then."

"I like Alex, Sophie. And I know you try to act tough, but I worry about you. That you'll get hurt."

It was early, and she'd had far too little sleep to listen to a lecture. Not to mention that she was a little worried herself. Something happened last night. Something…special. What was supposed to be just sex, felt like a heck of a lot more. To her at least. But what had Alex been thinking? And did she want to find out?

No way. They'd had one really good night together, and they would leave it at that, just as they had planned.

"There's really no need to worry," she told Hannah, then she gave both her and Frederick a kiss on the cheek. "I'll see you later tonight, at the ball."

"I just hope you know what you're doing," Hannah called after her.

So did she. She could not risk doing the one thing she swore she wouldn't.

Fall in love with him.

Alex watched Sophie from across the Royal Inn ballroom. She was dressed in a clingy, shimmering, floor-length gown suspended by two micro-thin spaghetti straps, and her hair was done up in a complicated-looking twist that showcased her long, graceful throat and narrow, deeply tanned shoulders. She glided from person to person, moving as eloquently as the orchestra that played in the background.

She managed to look elegant and refined, and sexy as hell at the same time.

Apparently she had been just what he needed, because he couldn't remember the last time he'd slept so soundly, when he hadn't woken with a dark cloud hanging over his head, a feeling of impending dread in his chest. He felt…at peace.

What he should have been feeling was some sort of satisfaction or triumph. He'd come here intending to seduce Sophie and he had. And even better, she had come to him. All he had to do now was leave her. And he knew he had her heart. He could see it in her eyes last night that she still loved him.

But there was a major kink in his plans. Now that he'd gotten to know her again, it was clear that she wasn't the woman he'd expected her to be. And the genius of his revenge plot now seemed petty and juvenile.

They had shared a car with Phillip and Hannah to the hotel, and Sophie did a damned fine job of pretending she and Alex hadn't spent the previous night in bed together. She was polite and as friendly as one might be with a colleague or business associate.

When they arrived at the Royal Inn, where the charity was being held, it was instantly clear to him the burden that the royal title could be for every member of the family. They were accosted by the press the instant they stepped from the car, then once inside, a flood of staff and guests monopolized them for what was going on two hours now.

Alex was content to sit at the bar and watch her. Every so often he would catch her eye and something would pass between them. A hungry look or a shared, secret smile, and he would know exactly what she was thinking. He couldn't escape the feeling that she was keeping her distance on purpose though.

"I don't believe we've met."

Alex turned to find a very attractive brunette sitting on the stool beside his. She wore a painted on, siren-red dress with a plunging neckline that she filled to capacity.

"Alexander Rutledge," he said, offering his hand.

"Madeline Grenaugh." Her handshake was soft and suggestive, and when she let go, she grazed his palm with nails that looked like blood-red claws. "You're an American."

"Guilty."

"East coast?" she asked.

"New York. You're good."

"Mr. Rutledge, you have no idea." She flashed him an overtly sensual smile. Man was she laying it on thick. Why not just drop a room key in front of him, or MapQuest directions to her house?

"What brings you to our fair country?" she asked.

"I'm a guest of the royal family, actually. I went to college with King Phillip."

"Then we have something in common. My family has been close friends with the royal family for years."

"Alex, there you are!"

He turned to see Sophie gliding toward him, her dress shimmering in the light of the chandeliers. The warm glow playing off all of those dips and curves he found so enticing.

"I'm sorry I haven't been much of a hostess," Sophie apologized, then glanced toward Madeline and with a polite smile said, "Oh, hello, Madeline, I didn't see you sitting there."

Alex had the feeling that Madeline was precisely the reason Sophie had taken the time to walk all the way across the room.

Madeline bowed her head and said, "Hello, Sophie."

She didn't address her by her title, which Alex suspected was an intentional slight. The tension they were giving off practically knocked him over.

"I see you've met our guest," Sophie said, laying a hand on Alex's arm. It was a territorial move. Her way of saying, *Back off, he's mine,* which was pretty funny coming from a woman who had made it very clear, on more than one occasion, that he *wasn't* hers.

"I have," Madeline said, reaching out to touch the hand he'd been resting on the bar, shooting him one of those inviting smiles. "We're finding that we have a lot in common. And I believe that he was just about to ask me to dance."

He was? And give her a chance to sink her claws in? Not in this lifetime. Sexy or not, the last thing he needed in his life was another manipulative female. Even if it was only for a five-minute twirl on the dance floor.

"I'm sorry, Madeline," he said, pulling his hand from under hers. "But I promised Princess Sophie the first dance." He rose from the bar stool. "It was nice to meet you, though."

If looks could kill. Her smile went from sizzling to arctic cold in the span of a heartbeat.

He offered Sophie his arm, and she slipped hers through it. Then she nodded and smiled to Madeline, twisting the knife. And obviously relishing it.

"You seemed to enjoy that," Alex said as he led her to the dance floor.

She put on her innocent face. "What do you mean?"

"Don't give me that. You looked as though you wanted to scratch each other's eyes out."

She cracked a smile. "Maybe I enjoyed it a little."

"You don't like her?"

"She's a vampire. And she's had her heart set on the

crown since we were children. She went after Phillip with a vengeance. When she realized that wasn't going to happen, she slept and manipulated her way through all of upper society. No intelligent man will go near her. She must have seen you and smelled fresh blood."

They stepped onto the dance floor, weaving through a throng of other formally dressed guests to an unoccupied spot in the center. He pulled her into his arms, and although he had expected her to put up at least a little resistance, she came willingly. A perfect fit against his arms, as though she belonged there.

Temporarily, of course.

"And I guess it had nothing to do with jealousy," he said.

She leveled her gaze on him. In heels, she stood nearly eye to eye. "And who would be the jealous one in this scenario?"

"You would."

She snorted indignantly. "You wish."

"I don't have to wish. I *know.* You were jealous."

She turned her nose up at him. "Your arrogance never ceases to amaze me."

He slid his hand from her waist, grazing the bare skin of her back with his fingertips, felt her shiver. With the slightest tug he drew her in just a little bit closer.

"Stop that!" she hissed. And even though her lips said no, her eyes were telling him to go for it.

He leaned forward, close to her ear, and whispered, "Admit it, Princess. You want me."

"I already *had* you," she whispered back.

"Yeah, but we both knew one night would never be enough." He nipped at the shell of her ear and a soft moan slipped from her lips. "Why fight it?"

"You're absolutely right, there must be an unoccupied closet around here somewhere. Or maybe we should just grab a room key and head upstairs."

He just grinned, because, joking or not, it might come to that. He stroked his thumb against her bare back. God, he wanted her. He wanted to put his hands on her. Peel that gown from her body and kiss every inch of her skin. "One more night, Princess. I'll make it worth your while."

"I fail to see how."

"Think multiples. Lots of them."

Her eyes warmed and a subtle grin curled the corners of her lips, and he knew she was his.

"I don't know about you, Your Highness, but I'm feeling *tense* again."

She tipped her head and gazed up at him through a curtain of dark lashes. "Are you really?"

"Yep."

"Well then, you know what that means." She glanced around to see if anyone was looking, then leaned forward, her lips brushing his ear, her breath hot on his skin, and whispered in a sultry voice. "You're going to have a really long night."

Twelve

Sophie hadn't been kidding when she said it would be a long night. And she'd made sure of it, by basically torturing him. Rubbing up against him on the dance floor when no one was looking, sliding her leg against his under the table during dinner or slipping her hand under the tablecloth to lay it on his thigh. And all with the rest of the family sitting at the table.

She was ruthless and she was good at it. By the time the second course was served he was so turned on he felt ready to crawl out of his own skin.

After dinner she excused herself to the ladies room and Alex headed straight to the bar for a drink. A strong one. With lots of ice that he may or may not dump down the front of his pants.

It was only eight, and according to Sophie they wouldn't be getting out of there any sooner than midnight. Possibly later. And then there was the problem of getting over to her residence unnoticed. Or maybe she would come to him again.

The bartender set his double scotch on the bar and Alex took a deep swallow.

"Can I have this dance?"

He turned to find Sophie standing behind him, that devilish look in her eyes.

"So you can torture me?"

She smiled. "You started it."

Yes, he had. And he was probably getting exactly what he deserved. And quite frankly loving the hell out of it. Not only was it sexually arousing, but he was having…fun. "Can you keep your hands to yourself? Miss We-Have-to-Be-Discreet."

She held out a hand to him. "I promise to behave."

He took her hand and let her lead him out to the dance floor. He seriously questioned her promise to behave, but if she had planned not to, she never got the chance. In the beginning of the first song, she slipped, and if he hadn't been holding on to her, she would have probably gone down hard on the dance floor. She let out a cry of pain, clutching his arms and holding one foot off the ground.

He steadied her, so she didn't fall over. "What happened?"

"My ankle. I think I twisted it."

"Are you all right?"

She winced and nodded. "I think so. My shoe fell off. Do you see it?"

He looked down and found it lying about a foot away. He leaned over and grabbed it for her, and saw immediately what had happened. The heel had partially snapped off. "It's broken."

"What?"

He handed it to her. "The heel busted."

Around them couples were beginning to stop and look and murmur words of sympathy. This had to be embarrassing for her, almost taking a dive on the dance floor. Not that he felt she had any reason to be embarrassed. Accidents happen. But Sophie liked to be in control, to be self-sufficient. This was the sort of thing that would really chap her pride.

"Can you put weight on it?" Alex asked, wanting to get her out of the crowd and back to the table before people started making a scene.

"I don't know." She put her foot flat on the floor and sucked in a surprised breath, her eyes welling with moisture. "Ouch."

That was a big *no.* "Let's get you back to the table."

She winced in pain. "I don't think I can walk."

He hadn't planned on making her walk, or hobble back on one foot. He scooped her up off her feet—or in this case, her *foot*—and into his arms. She gasped and looped her arms around his neck.

He carried her across the dance floor, the crowd parting like the Red Sea to allow them through. When

Hannah and Phillip saw them coming, they both flew to their feet.

"What happened?" Hannah rushed to Sophie's side as Alex set her down in her chair. "Are you okay?"

"I'm fine." She showed Hannah her shoe. "I twisted my ankle when my heel broke."

"Do you need a doctor?" Phillip asked.

Sophie rolled her eyes. "It's just twisted."

"It was probably that slippery dance floor," Hannah said. "I almost fell once, too."

"Then we should sue the owners for negligence," Sophie said. "Oh wait, that's *us.*"

Hannah knelt down and examined the ankle, and when she touched it, Sophie winced. "It's swelling," she told Phillip. "She needs to ice this. And probably have the physician look at it to be on the safe side."

"I'll escort her home," Phillip said.

"Phillip, this is your benefit," Sophie told him. "You can't just *leave.* Get me to the car and I'll be fine alone."

"I'm not sending you home in a car alone."

If there was a better time to jump in, Alex couldn't think of one. "You stay," he told Phillip. "I'll see her home."

"Are you sure?" Phillip asked.

Oh, yeah, he was sure. Sophie would definitely be needing some pampering, and he was the man for the job. Not that he believed it would go any further than that with her being in obvious pain.

He was seeing a very long, cold shower in his immediate future.

"Should we call for a wheelchair?" Hannah asked, looking worried.

"I can carry her," Alex said.

Sophie shot him a wry smile. "Are you sure? I wouldn't want you to hurt yourself."

"I'll manage."

Hannah said something to one of the bodyguards, then turned back to them. "They're pulling up a car around back, so this doesn't become a press spectacle. Or we'll be reading in the papers tomorrow that she has a compound fracture or her leg was severed."

With no effort at all, Alex scooped Sophie out of the chair and followed Hannah, trailed by Phillip and two stoic bodyguards, out the back door and through the kitchen to the service entrance. As promised there was a car waiting just outside the door. As well as a small crowd of photographers. So much for avoiding the press.

Under a shower of flashes, Alex set Sophie on the seat in the back and got her settled in, then turned to Phillip and Hannah.

"Make sure she takes something for the swelling," Hannah said. "And see that she keeps the ankle elevated."

"Thanks for taking care of her, Alex," Phillip said, shaking his hand. "We'll try not to be too late."

"No need to rush. I'm sure she'll probably take something for the pain and go right to bed."

"Well then, we'll see you tomorrow when we leave for the yacht."

The bodyguards escorted them back inside and Alex climbed in beside Sophie. "Well, that was exciting."

"You know me. Never a dull moment." She removed the unbroken shoe and tossed it, along with the broken one, on the seat beside her, and told the driver. "To the palace."

"Don't you want to go back to your residence?"

"I think it's better if we go to your suite."

Was she suggesting that she still wanted to spend the night together?

She pulled the pins from her hair and it tumbled down across her shoulders in a dark and silky cascade, and he felt mesmerized watching her.

"I figured you would want to go right to bed," he said.

She flashed him a sexy smile. "Oh, I do."

"Your *own* bed," he said. "To rest."

She shrugged. "I'm not tired."

"What about your ankle?"

"What about it?"

What about it? "Doesn't it hurt?"

She twisted it back and forth a few times, then rotated it in a circle. Then she stomped it down hard on the car floor. "Well, would you look at that. It seems to be all better."

All better? Wait a minute… "Your Highness, were you *faking* it?"

"How else were we supposed to get out of there?"

"What did you do? Go in the ladies' room and break off your heel?"

She just smiled.

He should have known. He should have figured that a broken heel was too damned convenient. So much for her worrying about her pride.

He folded his arms across his chest. "That's devious, even for you."

"I've done worse, believe me. And I would have told you, but I needed it to be convincing." She laid her hand on his thigh, gazing up at him with wide, innocent eyes. "Are you angry with me?"

He eyed her sternly. "Very."

She gave him a pout. "Really?"

"Oh, yeah." He caught her behind the neck and kissed her, long and slow and deep, nipping her lip before he let go. "In fact, the minute we're alone, I plan to punish you severely."

If a punishment to Alex meant satisfying a woman until she was limp and defenseless, then he'd made good on his threat.

She lay in bed beside him, their arms and legs entwined, her head resting on his chest. And she knew already that any further *one-more-night* talk was just pointless. She wanted a hundred nights with Alex. A thousand even.

But she would settle for the little time he had left.

She stroked his chest, playing with the fine, silky hair. "Can I ask you a question?"

"I guess that depends on the question."

"What was your wife like?"

"Oh, *that* kind of question. And here I was having such a good time."

"Come on, Alex, she couldn't have been *that* bad."

"She was…" He struggled with it for a moment, then finally said, "Ambitious."

"She worked?"

"Oh, no. She was very content to spend my money. When I say ambitious, I'm talking socially. She was friends with the right people and chair of all the right clubs. She drove the right car and lived in the right neighborhood. She was even having an affair with her personal trainer. Talk about socially acceptable."

"I didn't know that. I'm sorry."

"I wasn't. That was a sobering moment for me. Learning my wife was cheating on me and not giving a damn."

Sobering and sad. "You didn't care at all?"

"I know it sounds odd. I kept waiting to feel rage or revulsion or even hurt. But the only thing I managed to feel was relieved. I felt as though I finally had an excuse to leave."

"Why did you need an excuse?"

"When I figure that out, I'll let you know."

She was so much better off not having married anyone. What a terrible way to live. Just like her parents, and probably their parents before them. And here she had believed that that only happened among the royal crowd.

Alex deserved better than that.

"It must have been lonely, being married to a woman you didn't love."

He shrugged. "We led very separate lives. Those last few months I hardly ever saw her and we barely spoke."

She rose up on her elbow, so she could see his face. "Did you ever cheat on her?"

The question seemed to surprise him. "I'm not going to lie and say I wasn't tempted, but my attorney firmly advised me to not give her any ammunition. I was faithful until we were legally separated."

Put in the same situation, she wasn't sure if she would have had the patience to be faithful. Of course, she would have never married a man she didn't love.

"You know," he said, reaching up to trace her lips with his finger. "I've always found your accent incredibly sexy."

She smiled. "Not to be obtuse, but in this country you're the one with the accent."

"You're beautiful." He cupped her cheek, searching her face. She closed her eyes and leaned into his hand.

"This feels good," she said. "You and me."

"It does. I imagine that while I'm working on the fitness center I'll be visiting here rather often."

She cuddled back down against his chest. "I imagine you will."

"It would give us the chance to spend more time together."

Her heart caught in her throat. She wanted that more than he could ever imagine. She felt good when she was with him. She felt…normal. He was the only man she'd ever known who really seemed to get her. Who didn't take any of her crap. And even more important, he didn't try to overpower or smother her. He respected her independence. And it was right then she realized that despite swearing it would never happen, she loved him.

What the bloody hell had she done?

"Casually?" she asked, heart in her throat.

"Of course. I don't think either of us is looking for a commitment."

The string of disappointment was sharp and stinging, but what did she expect?

She shook her head. "I've come to the conclusion that I'm just too independent to be tied down." At least, she tried to tell herself that. Alex would be an automatic safety net.

She couldn't get herself caught up with a man who didn't want to be caught.

Thirteen

Alex stepped out of the shower and toweled off, then walked into the bedroom to check the time. He was supposed to meet Sophie downstairs in ten minutes for a walk in the gardens, and if he didn't hurry, he was going to be late.

He would be flying home in two days, back to the U.S., to his new life, the freedom he'd been dreaming of since the day he'd said *I do*—when what he should have been saying was *hell, no.* So why was it that the thought of leaving Morgan Isle left him with a hollow feeling in his gut?

The thought of spending more time here, opening an office in the bay area, held far more appeal than going back to New York. With all the renovation projects available, he wouldn't be short on work. And taking the company international had been his father's goal. Not that Alex would be doing it for anyone but himself.

Leaving in two days meant something else, too. It was nearly time to end things with Sophie. As far as he could tell, he'd done a pretty thorough job of making her fall for him. All that was left to do was dump her and break her heart. It sounded simple enough, but whenever he considered it, it never seemed to be the right time. He wasn't even sure what he would do or say.

But he was sure that eventually an opportunity would present itself.

His cell phone rang and he grabbed it off the bed and checked the display. It was Jonah. He felt as though he hadn't talked with him in months, instead of days.

"Sorry I haven't been in touch," Jonah said. "Crazy week. I just wanted to let you know that we got through moving day."

Funny, but Alex had completely forgotten about that. A week ago he'd been dreading the very idea of it, and now it just didn't seem all that important. He felt…removed from his old life.

Alex put the phone on speaker and set it on the nightstand so he could get dressed. "Did she try to pull anything?"

"Nothing that we weren't prepared for."

"Meaning what?" he asked, tugging on his pants.

"She didn't take anything that wasn't hers. And even better, you never have to so much as talk to her again."

His family wouldn't be happy about that. They were still holding out the hope that he would change his mind and reconcile with her, despite how many times he'd told them that wasn't going to happen.

Up until then, everything he'd done, every decision he'd made had been with someone else's needs and desires above his own. From now on he was doing what *he* wanted to do. Whether he had his family's blessing or not.

"Sounds like you've been having quite the time over there," Jonah said.

"What do you mean?"

"You're a celebrity."

Celebrity? "I'm not following you."

He laughed. "You really don't know, do you?"

He grabbed his shirt and tugged it on. "Know what?"

"Photos of you carrying the wounded princess are all over the media here."

"Seriously?" He'd been too busy lately to turn on the television or pick up a newspaper.

"Everyone is speculating whether or not you'll be the newest addition to the royal family."

Fat chance. Although the speculation would make his inevitable betrayal sting that much more. Which should have been a source of great satisfaction.

"I guess I don't have to ask how the revenge plot is panning out for you. It looks as though you have her eating out of the palm of your hand."

"Just as I planned," Alex said. So why did the thought leave him feeling…*hollow?*

"Well then, you must be feeling pretty good about yourself."

He should have been. He was getting exactly what he wanted.

He heard a sound from behind him and turned to see Sophie standing in the bedroom doorway. And he could see from her expression that she'd been there awhile.

He'd been looking for the right time and here it had found him.

"Jonah, I have to call you back." He grabbed the phone and snapped it shut, and Sophie just stared at him, her expression unreadable. He kept waiting for the feeling of satisfaction to sink in. To feel vindicated. He knew he should say something—this was his *big moment*—but his mind had gone blank.

Not Sophie's. She was never at a loss for the appropriate words.

"Don't bother trying to deny it," she told him. He couldn't tell if she was angry or hurt. She just sounded…cold.

"I wasn't going to." Why wasn't he rubbing this in her face? Twisting the knife?

"I guess it explains this," she said, holding out the tabloid newspaper he hadn't even noticed in her hand. On the cover was a black-and-white photo of Alex gallantly carrying Sophie from the ballroom, and above it in ridiculously large, bold type screamed the headline The Princess Stole My Husband!

"You neglected to mention that you and your wife were planning to reconcile."

When hell froze over. More likely, it was his ex's way of trying to screw with his life. Little did she know that by spreading her lies, she was actually helping him. Or she would be if he would only stick to the program.

What the hell was wrong with him?

"You're not going to deny that, either?" she asked.

He shrugged. "If it's in the tabloid, it must be true."

She let the paper slip from her grasp. It fluttered and separated, landing in sections on the carpet between them. If she was angry, or upset, she wasn't letting it show. She would never give him the satisfaction.

"You've been an entertaining distraction," she said, nose in the air. "Just as you were ten years ago. Although back then, you served a bit more of a purpose."

He'd heard this one before. "Your ticket to freedom?"

"My ticket to culinary school. It was simple, really. I dump you, my parents let me go."

That shouldn't have stung, but it did. Maybe because deep down he had wanted to believe her when she said she'd loved him, and that she had ended it for his sake. All this time he'd been forcing himself to see her as spoiled, self-centered. And now that she was proving him right, living up to his expectations, it just felt...*wrong*. This wasn't the Sophie he knew. This arrogant, entitled persona was just a defense.

"What's the matter, Alex? You look troubled." Her words dripped with icy disdain. "Was this not the reaction you'd expected? I told you, it was just sex. It's tough to get revenge on someone who doesn't care." She flashed him a look of pity. "Oh, Alex, you didn't honestly think I'd fallen for you again?" She cocked her head to one side. "Or is it that you've fallen for me?"

He didn't believe in hitting below the belt, but what he said next just slipped out. A swift, decisive jab where he knew it would sting the most. "You once told me that your parents were so cold, they made you believe that you were unlovable."

She lifted her nose in the air. "So?"

"Well, Princess, they were right."

Her expression didn't waver, but all the color leached from her face. She stood there for another few seconds, just staring at him, then without another word turned and walked from the room. In that instant he knew he'd won.

Only problem was, he was no longer sure what he was fighting for.

Sophie walked briskly down the stairs, a wash of unshed tears blurring her vision. If Alex had reached into her chest and ripped out her heart, it couldn't have hurt more. She'd let her guard down and trusted him. She'd been foolish enough to believe that he cared about her, too. These past eleven days she had been happy. She'd felt complete. But it had all been an act. A plot.

And she would die before she let him know how much he had hurt her.

As her foot hit the bottom step, she heard clapping from behind her. She snapped around to see Phillip descending the stairs behind her.

"Bravo," he said, his hands coming together in slow, sharp snaps that made her want to cringe. "That was some performance back there."

He'd obviously been eavesdropping. She had hoped he wouldn't find out about her and Alex, but there was little point in denying it now. "Mind your own business, Phillip."

He stopped on the step above her. "You are my business."

Again, why deny it, or bother to argue? Because he was right. He was the head of the family, and as such he would always have his nose in her business. She would think after thirty years she'd have accepted that. Maybe it was time.

"Are you angry?" she asked.

"I should be, what with you sneaking in and out of the palace at all hours. And that ridiculous fake twisted ankle."

He knew about that? And here she thought she had everyone, including him, fooled. She obviously didn't give Phillip nearly enough credit.

"But why would I be angry," he continued, "after working so bloody hard to get you two back together?"

Get them *back* together. She was so stunned by

his words her mouth fell open. "You knew about me and Alex?"

"I'd have had to be blind not to. When I brought him home from university, you two couldn't keep your eyes off each other. Then there were all the shared smiles and sneaking around."

"I thought I had everyone fooled."

"After he went back to America you were inconsolable, and honestly, Sophie, you haven't been the same since. It was like something died inside you. You just…gave up."

He was right. She had given up. The part of her that was capable of love and companionship had just shut down. And since then, no matter what she did, she never felt satisfied. She'd been searching for…*something*. Be it more responsibility or more respect. But maybe what had really been missing all this time was Alex.

He was the only man she'd ever loved. Maybe the only one she *could* love. Even if he could never love her back.

"So all that stuff you said about this being business, and my behavior being inappropriate. What was that?"

"The most effective way to make you go after something is to tell you that you can't have it."

Oh, that stung. Probably because he was right. Knowing he disapproved had given her that extra little shove she needed to set things in motion. Had he pushed Alex on her, she might have—probably would have—shunned him on principle.

Honestly, how did he put up with her?

"So all this time you've been playing me?" she asked.

He just smiled.

"What about Hannah? Was she in on it, too?"

"Of course."

They'd all had her fooled. Here she thought she had been in total control, but it was all just an illusion. They had been pulling the strings.

She should have been furious, but honestly, she was tired of fighting it. Tired of pushing so hard against the people who loved her most. A life that had been good to her, despite her constant complaining and moaning that she needed more.

She shook her head. "I can't believe that all this time you knew, but you never said anything."

He shrugged. "You're so bloody stubborn, I figured what's the point."

"And now?"

"Now I'm going to help keep you from making the second biggest mistake of your life." He took her hands and squeezed them. "Not so long ago I almost let the love of my life slip away, and you didn't hesitate to give it to me straight. In fact, I believe your exact words were 'You're an idiot, Phillip.' Well, now I'm going to return the favor." He took her by the shoulders and said firmly, "Sophie, you're being an idiot. And if you don't do something, you're going to lose him again. Tell him how you feel."

"What does it matter? You heard him. He was just using me."

"Do you honestly believe that?"

She no longer knew what to believe.

He might have started out using her, but something had changed. *He* had changed. At least, she'd thought so.

And if that was true, why hadn't he told her that? Why didn't he tell her that he'd made a mistake?

Because he didn't think that he had. And even so, what difference did it make? He would never be happy here with her, stuck in the royal lifestyle. It might be good for a while, but he would grow tired of her. People always did. He would see that she really was difficult and temperamental, and he would bail.

Phillip cradled her chin in his hand. "Do you love him, Soph?"

She shrugged. "What difference does it make?"

"It might make a difference to him."

She wished she could believe that. That she could take the chance. But one more direct hit to her pride might be more than she could bear.

"Sometimes getting what you want means taking risks," he said. "You taught me that."

But what if she wasn't sure *what* she wanted?

She did something then that she hadn't done in ages. She wrapped her arms around her brother and hugged him fiercely. "Thank you."

He squeezed her hard, resting his head atop hers.

"I love you, Sophie. I know I don't say it enough, and maybe I don't always show it. But I do."

"I love you, too, Phillip." She gave him one last squeeze, then let go.

He studied her for a moment, then said, "You're not going to talk to him, are you?"

She shrugged. "It was good advice. It's just not who I am." In fact, she wasn't even sure who she was these days. She wasn't sure if she had ever known. All she did know was, charade or not, when she was with Alex, she was happy. And when he was gone, she wasn't. And despite that, it wasn't meant to be.

That pretty much said it all.

Phillip gave his head an exasperated shake. "And you call me stubborn."

"Do me a favor? Don't say anything to him about this. Don't even let on that you know. And please don't let this affect your relationship with him. Business or personal. Promise me."

He hesitated, then nodded. "I promise."

"Thank you."

She turned to leave, and he called after her. "Stubborn as you are, I hope Alex has the good sense to try to work this out."

Honestly, so did she. But she wasn't counting on it.

Fourteen

Sophie barely slept that night, and spent the entire next day indoors to avoid any chance encounters with Alex. All the while praying that he would show up on her doorstep, ready to profess his undying love for her. She was both praying for it and dreading it with all her heart. Because like before, she would have to tell him no.

But Sunday evening, just as dusk fell, she watched from her office window as the car pulled around to the back of the palace and his bags were loaded into the trunk for the trip to the airport. She knew then, without a doubt, that it was over.

She felt heartsick clear through to the marrow of her bones, but relieved, too. It was easier this way. At least, that was what she would keep telling herself.

"I see that he's leaving," Wilson said from behind her.

Thankful for the distraction, she turned away from the window. To see Alex climb into the car and watch it drive away, knowing it was her own fault, would be more than she could take right now. "I guess he is."

"Are you sure, Your Highness, that it's for the best?"

Oh, God, not him, too. She sighed deeply and rubbed at the ache that had begun to throb in her temples. Couldn't anyone stay out of her business? "Wilson, you don't even like him."

"Perhaps I was a bit hasty when I drew that conclusion. And regardless of how I feel about him, he makes you happy."

But for how long? How long would it be before he broke her heart again?

Besides, she didn't have the energy for another argument about her love life. "I'm going to take a shower, then crawl in bed and sleep for a month. It would be fabulous if you'd not disturb me."

One brow tipped up. "For a month?"

She shrugged. "At least a solid ten or twelve hours."

He nodded, then backed out of the room. "As you wish, Your Highness."

He disapproved. He would never say it, of course, but she could tell. Why couldn't everyone trust that she knew what she was doing?

Sophie locked herself in the bathroom, stripped to

the skin, turned the shower on as hot as she could stand and stood there until the water ran cold. It was meant to relax her, but as she stepped out and toweled off, she felt just as tense and miserable as before. It felt as if something was missing, as though someone had reached deep inside her, grabbed hold of whatever it was that made her a whole person and snatched it away.

It was a sensation she remembered all too well. The same thing she'd felt the first time Alex had walked out of her life.

But to be fair, he hadn't walked so much as been shoved.

She wrapped herself up in a towel and stepped into her bedroom. The sun had set and the room was dark, so she switched on the lamp beside her bed. And nearly jumped out of her own skin when she noticed the dark figure standing across the room by the window.

In the instant it took to realize it was Alex, her heart had bottomed out all the way to the balls of her feet, then slammed upward to catch in her throat.

He turned to her, looking…actually, she couldn't say for sure how he looked. His face was expressionless.

"I was beginning to think you were never coming out," he said. "I guess you royals have no concept of water conservation."

She clutched the towel to her chest. This was odd to the point of being surreal. "I'm sure you didn't come here to discuss the environment. In fact, I'm curious as to how you managed to get past Wilson."

He tucked his hands into the pockets of his slacks and took a step toward her. "Gunpoint. He's tied up in the pantry."

She shot him a disbelieving look.

"Okay," he admitted with a shrug. "He let me in."

She might have been in the shower a long time, but certainly not the ten to twelve uninterrupted hours she had requested. Meaning she and Wilson were going to have to have a talk about following instructions, and him keeping his nose out of her business.

She glanced at the clock on the bedside table. "You're going to miss your flight."

"I'm not going to miss my flight, because I'm not planning on leaving."

Surely he didn't mean to say that he was staying for her. She lifted her chin, giving him the coldest look she could manage, when on the inside she was falling to pieces.

"Aren't you going to ask me why?"

She was afraid to. And whatever the reason, it didn't really make a difference.

He sighed. "You're not going to make this easy, are you?"

She raised her chin another notch and struggled to keep her voice even. "What do you want from me, Alex?"

"I came here to apologize."

Her heart did a swift backward flip. "For?"

"For calling you unlovable. Because you're not." He took a step toward her. "Ask me how I know that." When she didn't say anything he said, "Go ahead, ask me."

"How do you know?"

"Because *I* love you." He stepped closer, until he was right in front of her, and it took everything in her not to launch herself into his arms. "And I'm not going to let you run away from me again.

"Ten years ago I should have come after you, but I let my pride get in the way. And that's a mistake I'm not going to make again."

He reached out, touched her face, and that was all it took. Her heart slammed the wall of her chest and her knees turned to mush. And when he tugged her to him, she melted into his arms. She buried her face against his shirt, breathed him in. Clinging as if she never wanted to let go.

How could something so wrong feel so…perfect?

"You used me," she reminded him.

"And you used me. But at this point, does it really matter?"

No, not really. She looked up at him, into his eyes. "I hurt you, Alex, and I never once said I was sorry. And I am. I'm so, so sorry."

He smiled. "You're forgiven."

She laid her head on his chest, felt his heart beating against her cheek. "What if it doesn't work?"

He held her tight, stroked her damp hair. "How will we know if we don't try?"

"I'm stubborn and incorrigible. I drive everyone crazy."

He cupped her chin and tipped her face up to his. "Yeah, but all the things you do that drive me crazy are the things I love most about you." He lowered his head and kissed her. A sweet brush of his lips that was filled with affection and love. "You're perfect just the way you are."

She had waited all her life to hear someone say that. And she believed that he meant it. "I love you, Alex. I've never loved anyone but you."

He grinned down at her. "I know."

She laughed. "And you call *me* self-centered."

"Well," he said with a shrug, "you can't say we don't have anything in common."

"You know that this relationship could be a logistical nightmare. Transcontinental dating?"

"Then I'll have to move here."

"Oh, Alex, I can't ask you to make a sacrifice like that."

"You didn't ask. And it's not a sacrifice. In fact, I've been considering it ever since I got here. And for the record, I have no interest in dating you."

She frowned. "You don't?"

"For ten years, deep down I've known you're the one for me. And with all that time to make up, I think we should skip the dating altogether, and move right on to living together."

"Where?"

"Here, the palace. It's up to you."

"I'm not sure how the family will take that. It wouldn't be considered proper."

He sighed. "All right, then I guess you'll just have to marry me instead."

She was so stunned, her jaw nearly fell out of joint. "But you just got *un*married."

"I was never really married to her. Not in my heart. Unless you don't *want* to marry me."

Despite everything she'd said in recent years about never tying herself down to one person, about not wanting to sacrifice her freedom, being with Alex forever was no sacrifice. In fact, she couldn't think of a more perfect way to spend the rest of her life.

She smiled up at him. "Why don't you ask me and find out?"

He actually dropped on one knee, right there on her bedroom carpet, and took her hand in his. "Sophia Renee Agustus Mead, would you do me the honor of becoming my wife?"

"Yes," she said, with more joy than she ever thought possible filling her heart. "I will."

He smiled up at her. "Well, it's about damn time."

* * * * *

Don't miss
THE DUKE'S BOARDROOM AFFAIR,
the next book in
ROYAL SEDUCTIONS,
available January 2009
from Silhouette Desire.

Her breath whistled out in a sigh of relief when he exited Customs. Devon recognized him right away from the newspaper and magazine articles her friend and partner Sabrina had looked up during her frantic prep work.

Caleb John Logan, Jr. Thirty-one. Six-two. With jet-black hair, laser-blue eyes and a linebacker's shoulders under his charcoal-gray cashmere overcoat. His jaw-dropping good looks didn't score him any points with Devon. She'd learned the hard way not to trust handsome heartbreakers like Cal Logan.

But he was a client. An important one. And she was willing to give someone who'd served a hitch in the marines before earning a B.S. from the University of Oregon, an MBA from Stanford and his first million at the ripe old age of twenty-six the benefit of the doubt.

Right up until he spotted the hot-pink pashmina, that is.

Devon knew the flash of color was more visible than the sign she held up with his name on it. So she wasn't surprised when Logan picked her out of the crowd and cut in her direction. She'd just plastered on her best businesswoman smile when he whipped an arm around her waist. The next moment she was sprawled against his cashmere-covered chest.

"Hello, brown eyes."

Swooping down, he covered her mouth with his.

Sheer astonishment kept Devon rooted to the spot for a few seconds while her mind whirled chaotically. Her first thought was that her client had downed a few too many drinks during the long flight. Her second, that he'd mistaken the kind of escort and consulting services her company provided. Her third shoved everything else out of her head.

The man could kiss!

His mouth moved over hers with a skill that ignited sparks at a half-dozen flash points throughout her body. Devon hadn't experienced that kind of spontaneous combustion in a while. A *long* while.

The sparks were still popping when she pushed off his chest, only now they fueled a flush of anger.

"Do you always greet women you don't know with a lip-lock, Mr. Logan?"

A smile crinkled the skin at the corners of his eyes. "As a matter of fact, I don't. That was from Don."

"Huh?"

"He said he owed you one from New Year's Eve two years ago and made me promise to deliver it."

She stared up at him in total incomprehension. Logan hooked a brow and attempted to prompt a nonexistent memory.

"He abandoned you at the Waldorf. Five minutes before midnight. To deliver twins."

"I don't have a clue who or what you're…"

Understanding burst like a water balloon.

"Wait a sec. Are you talking about Sabrina's old boyfriend? Your buddy, who's now an ob-gyn doc?"

It was Logan's turn to look startled. He recovered faster than Devon had, though. His smile widened into a rueful grin.

"I take it you're not Sabrina Russo."

"No, Mr. Logan, I am *not.*"

* * * * *

HARLEQUIN
Blaze

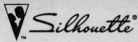

COMING NEXT MONTH

#1903 PREGNANT ON THE UPPER EAST SIDE?—
Emilie Rose
Park Avenue Scandals
This powerful Manhattan attorney uses a business proposal to seduce his beautiful party planner into bed. After their one night of passion, could she be carrying his baby?

#1904 THE MAGNATE'S TAKEOVER—Mary McBride
Gifts from a Billionaire
When they first met, he didn't tell her he was the enemy. But as they grow ever closer, he risks revealing his true identity and motives, and destroying everything.

#1905 THE CEO'S CHRISTMAS PROPOSITION—
Merline Lovelace
Holidays Abroad
Stranded in Austria together at Christmas, it only takes one kiss for him to decide he wants more than just a business relationship. And this CEO always gets what he wants.…

#1906 DO NOT DISTURB UNTIL CHRISTMAS—
Charlene Sands
Suite Secrets
Reunited with his ex-love, he plans to leave her first this time—until he discovers she's pregnant! Will their marriage of convenience bring him a change of heart?

#1907 SPANIARD'S SEDUCTION—Tessa Radley
The Saxon Brides
A mysterious stranger shows up with a secret and a heart set on revenge. Then he meets the one woman whose love could change all his plans.

#1908 BABY BEQUEST—Robyn Grady
Billionaires and Babies
He proposed a temporary marriage to help her get custody of her orphaned niece, but their passion was all too permanent.

SDCNMBPA1008